CAPTURED BY THE BRATVA

AVA GRAY

ALSO BY AVA GRAY

3 SEAL Daddies for Christmas
Small Town Sparks
Her Protector Daddies
Her Alpha Bosses
The Mafia's Surprise Gift

The Billionaire Mafia Series
Knocked Up by the Mafia
Stolen by the Mafia
Claimed by the Mafia
Arranged by the Mafia
Charmed by the Mafia

Alpha Billionaire Series
Secret Baby with Brother's Best Friend
Just Pretending
Loving The One I Should Hate
Billionaire and the Barista
Coming Home
Doctor Daddy
Baby Surprise
A Fake Fiancée for Christmas
Hot Mess
Love to Hate You - The Beckett Billionaires
Just Another Chance - The Beckett Billionaires
Valentine's Day Proposal
The Wrong Choice - Difficult Choices
The Right Choice - Difficult Choices
SEALed by a Kiss
The Boss's Unexpected Surprise
Twins for the Playboy
When We Meet Again
The Rules We Break

Secret Baby with my Boss's Brother
Frosty Beginnings
Silver Fox Billionaire
Taken by the Major
Daddy's Unexpected Gift
Off Limits
Boss's Baby Surprise
CEO's Baby Scandal

Playing with Trouble Series:
Chasing What's Mine
Claiming What's Mine
Protecting What's Mine
Saving What's Mine

The Beckett Billionaires Series:
Love to Hate You
Just Another Chance

Standalone's:
Ruthless Love
The Best Friend Affair

PARANORMAL ROMANCE

Maple Lake Shifters Series:
Omega Vanished
Omega Exiled
Omega Coveted
Omega Bonded

. . .

Everton Falls Mated Love Series:
The Alpha's Mate
The Wolf's Wild Mate
Saving His Mate
Fighting For His Mate

Dragons of Las Vegas Series:
Thin Ice
Silver Lining
A Spark in the Dark
Fire & Ice
Dragons of Las Vegas Boxed Set (The Complete Series)

Standalone's:
Fiery Kiss
Wild Fate

BLURB

He took me as his hostage. Now I'm falling for my silver fox captor.

I'm a single mother with everything to lose.
 My daughter is my whole world.
 I'd do anything to protect her.

But **him**?

Ivan Valkov. The Bratva's most lethal enforcer.
 Dangerous. Commanding. **Irresistibly mature**.
 He kidnapped me to get to my father.
 When he discovered my secrets, I expected brutality.
 Instead, this silver-streaked warrior became our shield.

Now we're **in his fortress**. Under his protection. In his bed.
 My daughter's giggles fill his dark world with light.
 But shadows are closing in. A sinister plot that **threatens to destroy us all**.

He thinks I'll run from him.

He's wrong.

Someone's watching. Waiting. Ready to strike.

My corrupt father. The rival mafia. A ghost from my past who won't stay dead.

The truth could tear us apart... or get us killed.

Because Ivan's given me something I never thought I'd find again.

A chance to **trust**.

In his world, love is a weapon.

And for my family, **I'll pull the trigger**.

Captured by the Bratva is a gripping, emotional mafia romance featuring a silver fox protective hero, a fierce young single mother with deadly secrets, and enough white-knuckle suspense to keep you breathless until the final page. Content advisory for mature themes.

1

IVAN

Standing toward the back of the reception space, I glanced over the guests mingling throughout the area. Unease crept up my spine. I couldn't shake it. This sensation of looking in from the outside set deep inside me, and it made no sense.

All the guests dancing, talking, and laughing here were acquaintances of the Valkov Bratva. This celebration of my brother Nickolai marrying Amy was a day to be shared with friends and family. I belonged here, but I couldn't chime in with the idea behind it all.

Marriage? It wasn't in the cards for me. I knew that down to my core. Nor would I ever be the groom over there, at the head table, smiling and kissing the one woman who'd be mine and only mine forever.

Monogamy was a goal, but as of yet, I had no reason to give up my preferences for staying unattached and focused on serving my family. Someone had to handle the Bratva's sex clubs. They turned too hefty of a profit to shut them down, and with Aleksei taking over as the *Pakhan*, he was all about increasing our wealth and power.

I just couldn't see it, standing around in a tuxedo, showing off the one woman who'd be at my side forever. I couldn't envision being a groom at a big, fancy reception like this, smiling and—

I furrowed my brow.

Wait a second.

Watching Nik frown further, I wondered what had made him take a call now. Amy peered at him, but I had to give her credit. She didn't pout or make a fuss out of it. She was a nobody before she met Nik, but she was proving her worth as a true Bratva woman, not interfering with our business.

I wasn't the only one who'd noticed Nik's reaction to whatever call he'd deemed so important that he had to take at his own wedding reception. Stepping further away, he tipped his chin at Alek who, like me, watched Nik. All five of us brothers were forever alert, even today at a highly guarded celebration.

Now what? Nik and Amy had a hard enough time getting to this peaceful and sappy day of matrimony. If anyone was trying to stir trouble, they'd have hell to pay.

Alek reached Nik first. We moved off to the side to speak, and I waited for Nik to hang up.

"That was Yusef." He looked past me, likely checking on Amy as he scowled and rubbed his face. "I asked him to keep an eye on Murphy's whereabouts."

At the name of that fucker, I gritted my teeth. Steven Murphy, crooked cop extraordinaire. He'd worked for the NYPD for his whole career, and he'd made it known that he wanted to be the one to bring the Valkov Bratva down.

"Nik. It's your wedding…" I said with a heavy sigh. "And I already told you. I'll handle Murphy." And I would. I volunteered to bring that asshole down, but it seemed Nik struggled to let go of it. My older brother actually would be better for this job. Nik was stealthy, skilled with disguises and hiding and spying. I'd stepped up at our previous meeting, though, because even if he wasn't a man newly in love with the woman he almost lost several times, he was also a father-to-be.

"I know. I know." He held up his hand and waved it at me. "But Yusef still reports to me. I'll tell him to address you from here on."

Alek crossed his arms. "What did he say?" He was straight to business, as ever. He knew he could count on all of us to pull our weight and get things done, but he was extra eager to stop Murphy from messing with us anymore.

"He's been hiding," Nik answered.

As he should be. If the cop knew I was about to be on his ass, he should be trying to hide or run. Our previous *Pakhan* was an idiot who abused and lost power, but under Alek's hand, we'd remind everyone that the Valkovs were an enemy no one should dare to cross.

"After we busted up that branch of the Ortezes' trafficking operation, Murphy's been hiding," Nik said.

Alek nodded, sighing. "Yeah. We overheard him talking with someone about getting a cut. I bet he's still trying to get something from the traffickers, just not with the Cartel anymore."

"I agree." Nik glanced in Amy's direction again, as though he hated to be away from her on this special day. "We interfered with that specific line of business, but he's still involved. It seems that Murphy's distancing himself from the Cartel, though."

I narrowed my eyes. "For good?"

Nik shrugged while Alek shook his head.

"He's got his hands in a little bit of everything," Alek replied. "He always has. I doubt that asshole has ever been a clean cop. As soon as he started on the force, he's been crooked. Don't you remember Dad trying to tell Pavel about his concerns?"

I thought back, trying to recall whatever memories Alek was referencing. Thinking about our father wasn't pleasant. He'd been taken from us too soon, and I hated the pang of grief that lingered despite all the years that had passed. We were only teens, young men, when Pavel arranged for our father to be killed. Pavel had wanted all the power of the Bratva, and even though our father was the smarter, more level-headed man with a brain and heart for leadership, Pavel was too greedy and coveted it all.

While I didn't remember any particular warning our father might have shared with us about Murphy, it wouldn't have shocked me if he'd only confided in Alek—the oldest—about his worries.

"He's not loyal about which crime organization he caters to," Alek added, rubbing his jaw and seeming more than irritated about this topic.

"No shit," I agreed. "First, he teamed up with Sergei Kastava to fuck us over at the Colver dock with that arms shipment and the sting that he prevented from happening."

They both nodded, grumpy about the reminder.

"Then, he collaborated with the Ortezes to attack our businesses."

Nik raised his brows at me. "And also wanted to continue getting a cut of the trafficking operation as it continues elsewhere within the Cartel."

"And that's just this year," Alek complained. "It's time to finish him once and for all."

I didn't cower under his direct stare with those words. I heard him. And I'd damn well take care of it.

"But Yusef seems to think Murphy's angling with the Rossinis now."

I rolled my eyes. *Those fucking Italians.* "Haven't they all killed each other by now?" All of the Families battling for power in New York suffered from infighting, but not as often as the Rossinis did.

"Yusef seems to think that this isn't anything new," Nik added. "Murphy's hiding, but with the tracking software Dmitri arranged for Yusef, there is a long record of correspondence with members of the Rossini organization."

Nothing seemed off about that. Murphy was an opportunist. He'd dance from one group to another, wherever he could count on the best benefits and rewards. Loyalty wasn't a part of that cop's makeup. He wasn't loyal to his job, any of the "bad guys" he was supposed to bring down. No one. Steven Murphy was a solo operator, and that would make finding him that much harder. If he was so flaky and two-timed his associates and connections, no one would want to offer him refuge and help him hide.

"I bet he's got records of talking with all kinds of people," I said.

"True," Nik replied, "but Yusef is starting to piece together a long track of correspondence with the Rossinis, even before the worst periods of their infighting and own drama."

"Maybe a long-standing scheme, then," I guessed. It hardly mattered what the asshole was doing. Whatever Murphy was up to, it was about to come to a stop when I ended his life.

Alek sighed, looking over the guests at the party. Even though we were over here talking about business, we all three tried to keep our expressions as neutral as possible. Mila, Alek's wife, was sentimental and emotional about this wedding. Both Mila and Amy were prone to the effects of hormones wrecking their bodies and minds. They'd cried throughout the events of the day, and I knew those pregnant women would be even more upset if they knew we were talking about missions and hard jobs over here.

"I'll contact Yusef," I told them both, eager to wrap up this conversation. It wasn't the time nor place for it. "And it doesn't matter what that fucker is planning with whoever he wants to pretend he's friends with." The Ortez Cartel wouldn't mess with us anytime soon. The Kastava Family had been cut down with the death of their leader. If Murphy wanted to bring me into some stupid plan with the Rossinis, so be it. "Regardless of any plans Murphy's making, he'll always be the enemy and no one will be able to protect him." He'd made his bed as a crooked cop, and he'd damn well lie in it.

Alek clapped his hand on my back. "Good."

"The Rossinis are never easy to follow, though," Nik said. He didn't react to my optimistic, get-it-done comment. Even though he was a married man, house hunting and committed to the preparations for being a father, he seemed to struggle with letting go of this enemy.

"But it's a start." I watched him closely, curious whether he'd struggle to let me handle this one for the family. "And I'll focus on looking into whatever he might be planning with the Rossinis and root that fucker out from wherever he's hiding."

Nik pressed his lips together and exhaled through his nose.

"No one can hide for good." I smoothed down my shirt and straightened my cuffs. "Not when the Valkov Bratva has targeted them." *Especially me.* Pavel used to brag that I was one of the most vicious killers they had in the family. No one ever wanted to cross me, and no one ever interfered with my preference for the darkness. At the sex clubs. At the scene when someone had to be tortured or killed. I was the sick fucker of us all, and I wouldn't suggest that anyone forget that anytime soon.

"Leave this one to me, Brother." I patted his shoulder, then gestured to the party. "Enjoy your wife." A glance at Alek showed he was smirking. "You too."

Alek scoffed, shaking his head. "Just see that you don't get sidetracked like Nik and I did."

I doubted he meant it. Meeting Mila and making her his wife wasn't an accident of being sidetracked. Alek loved his wife, and I had no doubt he was grateful for her in his life, her and their unborn daughter.

Nik chuckled wryly. "We're all getting distracted with women lately."

Speak for yourselves. "Not me." I'd made my peace with my future. A lifetime of bachelorhood was all I had to count on, and even though I felt like the odd one out here, without a plus-one or even any interest to chase a woman at the party, I was fine with that.

I'd never find a woman who'd suit my dark needs. Someone who'd welcome my rough attitude and need for pain. Who'd accept me for who I was and not try to change me into something softer and domesticated.

"No worries on that count," I told my skeptical brothers.

"Never say never," Alek warned.

I smirked at him. He had no room to tease me. As the leader, he would have been forced to settle with someone at some point.

"You don't know when it could happen," Nik taunted good-naturedly.

"More like *if* that would ever happen. And it won't."

Because there's no way in hell a perfect woman is waiting out there for someone like me.

2

BECCA

nother group passed by me, seeking out the trio of large canvases on the far wall. The gallery was packed, and that was good news. This opening-night showing was a success, but I couldn't claim the majority of it.

I sighed, smiling at the guests and wishing they'd meander toward the back. My Impressionist-style paintings hung back there, but only a few of them stood out within this multi-artist display.

Morgan was the focal point of the show, and while I was happy for my friend, I couldn't tamp down this stubborn sadness that lurked within my heart.

If I could have an inkling of her success, a small smidgen of all this fanfare and fame...

"Oh, excuse me," a woman said, interrupting my morose mood as she tried to squeeze through the crowd. Then she stopped, doing a double-take on me. "Wait. Aren't you...?"

I beamed, elated that she'd recognize me. All six of us participating artists had tiny thumbnail photos on the back of the pamphlet. Of course, Morgan took up a full half-page, her image in color and a paragraph of a biography rather than a one-liner about who she was. But this woman. She recognized *me*!

"Oh, wait. No." She flipped her paper over and smiled. "Sorry. I was looking for the painter of that landscape over there."

I kept my polite smile plastered on my face as she pointed at Morgan's face on the glossy pamphlet this woman picked up at the entrance. "Oh. Um, no, that's not me. Morgan is up there." Aiming my finger at the excited crowd that surrounded Morgan toward the front of the gallery, I fought the rising burn of envy.

Jealousy wasn't becoming. I knew that. I didn't usually sink to that lowness. And I tried my damnedest to squash it all. I wasn't *jealous*. I couldn't call myself a real artist if I envied another painter's style. My style was my own, and I'd never change it.

Still, I struggled with the challenge of this envy of my friend's success.

Stop. You'll have your moment someday. I turned away, gripping the clay pendant on my necklace for comfort. My grandmother crafted this smooth shape, and every time I rubbed it between my thumb and finger, I felt connected to her. That my grandma's artistic inspiration couldn't fail me forever. That nothing lasted forever, the good or the bad, and I'd been dealt a fair share of *badness* in my twenty-five years on this earth.

I walked back toward my pieces, eyeing the selection of small sculptures arranged under bright lights. Paintings were easier to get credit for, but the gallery owner had rudely insisted on "quantity over quality," making a case for showing several of my sculptures since they didn't take up too much space in the rooms. A variety of art media was preferred, and I spent more concentration on my sculptures than my paintings.

Hey, I'll take it. Even though none of my artwork was getting much attention here, it *was* here, and that was something to be proud of.

If my life were more like Morgan's, I bet I'd be able to go further with my art. As a single mother of a ten-month-old, working a crappy job for a courier company, and without any family or support, I was limited in how much time and effort I could dedicate to my passion. Morgan was single, childless, and from a wealthy family with connections. It was no wonder she'd gotten far.

The only connection I had was my scummy, lying father.

And Dom.

I winced as I walked around, trying to look relaxed and not tense. Dominic Rossini had once appeared to be a connection who could have really led me to fame in the art world. He'd doted on me, dating me and making me feel special for so long, only to reveal his true intentions. That distinguished Italian strung me along only as a way to get closer to my father. For months, Dom conned me, making me think he loved me and my artwork with his vague plans to sponsor me in Italy and get me into European galleries. All that time, I thought I'd hit the jackpot in finding an older gentleman who cared about my artwork.

Instead, I learned he led a double life as a crime lord who'd simply pursued me as a way to maintain some kind of a business arrangement with my father.

It was all a lie.

Just thinking about Dom soured my stomach, but it wasn't as awful as the headache that grew as I thought about my finances. I only had so much to pay Hannah for babysitting Emily tonight, and I felt so selfish to pay for childcare that didn't amount to my working and picking up extra hours.

I hope she's not being finicky. At the thought of my sweet girl, I smiled and wondered if Hannah was having any luck with her. *Teething time sucks.* It was brutal, and I wondered when that first tooth would cut through already and end Emily's consistent fussiness.

I pulled my phone out of my purse, smiling and glancing around to see if anyone would notice. Being glued to a screen was a huge mistake to make here. I had to be *on*, smiling and chatting, promoting the showing and my artwork, socializing and mingling.

But simply seeing the screensaver of my baby calmed me. Emily was the brightest ray of sunshine in my life, and I vowed daily to do my best for her.

The text thread with Hannah showed nothing new, but then again, the college-aged sitter seldom complained. She was too sweet and competent to ever struggle with Emily.

Before I could stash my phone back in my purse and resume this smiling, fake-it-'til-you-make-it peppiness, the device buzzed with an incoming call.

Shit. Taking a call would be a bigger transgression. Once I saw that it was my dad, though, I sighed and knew he'd continue to call until I answered. I didn't want to deal with his pushiness, so I stepped aside to settle whatever he wanted.

I missed the call in the time it took me to find a spot near the drinks in the back of the gallery, but sure enough, he called again.

Steven Murphy never called to check in. Or see how I was doing. The fact that he called back to back without a pause meant he wanted something.

What's new? He always wanted something.

"Hey, Becca," he answered quickly, stuffing enough charm to make it seem like a personal call. He didn't give a shit about me. I wouldn't be conned. Not by him.

"Are you busy?"

I looked around the gallery, smiling in case anyone saw me. "Yes." No one was here to speak with me about my art, but I clung to the chance that someone could.

"I need you to come to my place and talk about reaching out to Dom."

I blinked. Then blinked some more, wondering if I misheard. "Dom?"

"Yeah. Dominic Rossini," he replied snarkily. "Don't tell me you forgot about your boyfriend already."

Dom never really *was* my boyfriend. He'd tried to act like one, but he never cared about me like a real significant other would have.

"He contacted me, wanting to talk about custody for Emily."

I snorted, shaking my head and losing the smile for the crowd here. There was no chance in hell I could mask this scowl. No one was looking at me, anyway.

"The hell he is," I retorted. My dad calling me to arrange a discussion wasn't a bizarre thought. I'd met Dom through my dad. But his claim was bullshit. "Dom never acknowledged Emily. He was never even aware that I was pregnant."

I didn't give him a chance to cajole me any further. Anger rose too quickly and hotly. "What do you want, Steven?"

Calling him *Dad* never happened. He wasn't a father figure, so it hadn't even felt natural to refer to him as such.

"Well, first to see how you're doing and all..." His tone fell into that cunning, persuasive sugariness, and I rolled my eyes.

I was far too used to his lies to fall for this. "What do you want?" I repeated bluntly.

"I just want to see how my baby girl is doing."

"No, you don't." I was calling his bluff.

"Listen, I've got a lot of things going on with work."

Like I haven't heard that excuse before.

"And I feel like I'm not available for you like I want to be."

You never have.

"I feel guilty about being such a workaholic."

"I don't have time for this." I was too jaded to be patient and give him a chance. "I'm hanging up."

"Fine. Wait."

I shook my head, so bitter that I considered changing my number. Actually, I had done that before, when I was eighteen and wanted to cut all ties with him when he asked me for money. As a cop, though, he'd found me anyway.

"I need you to go to this sex club and ask for someone for me."

I snorted. "What?" *A sex club?* "No way."

"I can't go myself. I'd be recognized as law enforcement in that crowd."

I didn't even want to put the idea of my father and a sex club together. *Eww.*

"My cover wouldn't hold up there."

"Then ask one of your colleagues." Was he insane? He had to be to ask me to do him a favor like this. All my life, he'd wanted favors from me, and I knew how poorly those tended to end up.

"That's not a great idea," he argued.

Oh, he'd ask his daughter to be an accomplice with something at a sex club—a place I'd never consider visiting to begin with—but not his fellow officers. That right there told me this was another one of his corrupt plans, and I wanted nothing to do with it.

"Someone will have an envelope for me there. I just need you to get it and deliver it to me."

"No. *Hell* no. I don't trust you."

"Okay." He huffed. "Then I'll tell Dom how to reach you so he can talk to you directly about this custody business."

I narrowed my eyes, fuming and trying to find the fewest words to reply. He was threatening me, his own flesh and blood. The fact that he'd stoop so low to threaten me infuriated me. This was nothing but an ultimatum, but I wasn't worried. I doubted Dom knew I had his baby. And he wouldn't have cared.

"You're lying." I shook my head and turned, giving the gallery crowd my back as I glowered at the wall. "And I'm *sick* of it."

All my life, he'd looked out for himself, trying to score money and power. Not once did he ever care about me, and I was so damn tired of his attempts to control me.

"I'm not helping you with a single fucking thing, Steven."

Then I hung up, pushed too far past my quota of patience to hear his voice. Pressing my fingertip on the screen to end the call did little to appease my anger. Scathing mad and annoyed, I drew in a deep breath and tried to get back into the spirit of being here.

It was hopeless. Once I caught my breath and slapped on what I hoped was a smile, I replayed the conversation in my head with the repeated awareness of what it all meant.

Control. Steven only wanted to manipulate me, to use me for his own gains.

Just like Dom had.

Zoning out on the crowd that praised Morgan's artwork and not anyone else's, I sank into a pit of despair, wishing this wasn't how my life had to be.

Never mind my artwork. Most days, it felt like a pipe dream to wish for success in that field.

With a deeper sense of longing, I wished—not for the first time—that I could find someone who would care about *me*. Just the way I was. With no expectations or rules to follow. No burdens or obligations. No roles or chances of being used for something else.

Someone to love and support me, no matter what.

Keep dreaming, Bec. Keep fucking dreaming...

3

IVAN

Surveillance was Nik's forte, but I'd handled searching for plenty of people too. We all did in our efforts to keep the Valkov Bratva strong and secure.

But finding Murphy proved to be harder than I thought it might be, and I hated that I'd underestimated my ability for rooting out the cop.

For over a week, I tried and failed to get a bead on where the officer was hiding. Officially, he'd taken a sabbatical from work. Informants verified that he'd put in paperwork with his superiors to have time off. Unofficially, he was taking cover and making my life difficult.

Yusef was a big help on the streets, tracking leads that took him nowhere. I tasked soldiers to remain alert near all the addresses we'd ever had for Murphy. He was slippery, changing residences often, but he didn't show up at any of them.

Despite all the manpower I arranged to help me find Murphy, my only stroke of fortune was in the tracking software Dmitri handled most often. My younger brother showed me all the arrangements he and Yusef had set up to rifle through the calls Murphy had made. Most calls were to numbers associated with burners. Messages were encrypted, and the calls couldn't always be traced. When they were accurately traced, the locations of the callers moved constantly.

My frustration scaled so high that the usual peace I found at the sex clubs didn't make a dent on my mood. I was too pissed, thwarted, and impatient to have to struggle in hunting down Murphy.

The day a pattern showed up, though, I warned myself not to be too optimistic and get my hopes up high.

"Same number," Yusef confirmed. He scrolled on the monitor at the mansion my uncle Pavel used to live in. Since Alek took over, he'd made it the Bratva headquarters. Upstairs, we lived and held meetings, parties too. Downstairs, the labyrinth of secret rooms housed all kinds of surveillance equipment. Maxim was trying to find more hackers, but they were fickle, almost like Murphy was—not willing to be loyal to any one provider. Opportunists at heart.

I narrowed my eyes, watching as he showed me the number Murphy often called. "Who is it?"

He shrugged, yawning from a long spell of sitting at the desk down here. "I think his daughter."

"Daughter?" I glanced at the man. Hearing that Murphy had a kid came as a shock.

"Yeah. Becca Murphy. Here's what I could find on her." He handed over some print-outs. As far as a file went, hers was slim. The photo of her was grainy, taken from a security camera at an office, but her driver's license image was clearer.

Red hair, green eyes. An Irish beauty, even with the unmissable fatigue in her gaze as she tried to smile for her identification photo.

"Thanks." I skimmed the rest of the information we had on her, committing the slight collection of facts to memory. Yusef found a current address for her, as well as a location of her employment. Armed with those two destinations, I got ready to follow her until I knew how I could grab her.

After what happened with Amy—when the Cartel snatched her off the sidewalk to sell her to a creepy fucker named Diego—I faced a morsel of unease about planning to stalk Becca.

As a rule, we didn't sell women. Human trafficking wasn't a path

Alek wanted to take the Bratva down. Guns and drugs were lucrative enough, not to mention the clubs and brothels.

And I wasn't planning to *keep* this girl. Taking this woman was unavoidable. She was the only clear method I had to get Murphy's attention. Holding her hostage should do the trick. If Murphy had cared enough to make a daughter and give her his name, then he had to hold her in some kind of high regard and to want her safe and happy.

Seeing Alek and Nik prepare for fatherhood, I knew that the idea of having a child changed a man. My brothers were ruthless killers, but they had good hearts. They would be great fathers, and I assume that might hold true for Murphy as well. People would be quick to consider all of us in the Bratva as bad men, and I was aware of just how corrupt and crooked Murphy was. He really was the villain.

I relied on Murphy to come running as soon as I had Becca, and with that step plotted out in my mind, I got busy figuring out how to make it happen.

For several days, I followed her from a distance. I stalked her until I could get a feel for her predictable routine, for how and when she'd be most vulnerable to be taken away.

It was all too easy. She was a workaholic, always reporting to work at a courier office. For the number of hours she put in, she had to be doing decently for money, yet she resided in a shithole of an apartment in a crappy part of town.

Doubts filtered into my mind.

If Murphy cares about her, wouldn't he help her move into a better place?

If he's worried about her working so much, wouldn't he loan her some money?

I shook my head at that thought. Murphy was a greedy fucker, always trying to get his hands on riches, usually at the cost of the Bratva or another crime organization in the city.

Maybe he's too selfish to care about Becca being held hostage.

If that was the case, I knew I could push a little harder. Incriminating evidence of her being taken against her will would do the trick. And I was a sick enough bastard to pull that off. Never minding what

Alek and Nik teased, I wasn't going soft for a pretty woman, not anytime soon.

Besides, the redheaded, freckled-skin, green-eyed beauty was not *pretty*. She was gorgeous in a timeless, effortless way that warned me against getting excited about taking her.

She looked innocent. Soft. Delicate.

Not hardened enough to handle the way I would like to fuck.

Assuming that she was that good and sweet, I planned to set her out of her comfort zone and make it easier for me to steal her away.

"You ready?" I asked Dmitri as he prepared to leave the mansion with me.

He nodded. "Always."

We rode together for this first step to be put into action. It was all too easy to arrange for a delivery to take place at one of the Bratva's sex clubs. While she performed her duties as a courier, dropping off a decoy of a small document package there, I'd guide her to a false exit and take her to my place.

The residential complex I owned near Brooklyn was secure enough for holding her hostage. The walls were soundproofed, and the doors and windows were alarmed. No one would get in or out, and I figured bringing her there would be adequate. I wouldn't need to torture her. I didn't have to plan on killing her and punishing her.

Keeping her captive would be enough. Murphy *would* reveal himself. He had to.

Murphy's dedication to lying low alarmed me, and it seemed I wasn't the only one thinking along that line of caution.

"What do you think he's planning?" Dmitri asked as he drove us to the club. He'd be there as backup, not that I needed it. This club was part of my responsibility to supervise. More than anything, it seemed my brother was bored and wanted in on the case.

"Something bad if he's hiding this well that we can't find him," I replied.

"Exactly."

"And if it's something bad…" I furrowed my brow. "It's probably going to impact us."

Dmitri scoffed. "He's had a hard-on to end us forever."

He won't. "Which means it's time to take him out, once and for all."

After we entered, he left my side and blended into the background. He didn't visit the clubs often, and I wasn't surprised when he kept to the bar area rather than circulating through the open floor area where scenes were played for anyone wanting to watch.

I checked my watch, knowing the moment was here. Stalking Becca showed me that she visited a variety of locations while she was on the clock, but I bet if she had a hunch she would be delivering something to a top-secret sex club like this, she might not have agreed to see the duty done.

Fortunately, the address was hard to find, and because of that, I didn't worry when she showed up late. I'd informed all the guards to look out for her and to let her in.

Eyes opened wide with alarm and confusion, she entered the main lobby space of the sex club and stared at it all. The toys. The nudity. The collars. I tracked her coming through the room as she roved her head from side to side as she took it all in.

Imagining it from her sheltered perspective, I tried to experience it through her senses.

Seeing the woman whipped while strapped to a cross.

Hearing another pair of women moaning filthy sounds of pleasure as men shared them in an orgy.

Smelling the potent tang of sex hanging in the air.

A floor monitor approached her, and Becca flinched at someone speaking to her. She held up the manilla package, and I watched as she explained to the staff member that she was here to deliver something to me. I'd listed myself as the fake client she was supposed to find, and I waited expectantly as she was directed to me, the staff member pointing me out.

"Excuse me? Are you Mr....?"

I turned toward her, hit with the full effect of her innocent beauty this close. Instead of following her from a distance and staking out near her residence, I was right here with her. Feet apart.

No makeup hid her beauty from me. No pretenses of a shy subbie looking for a good time at a club. She was on the clock, assuming this was work as usual for her, and it allowed me a chance to let her sexy innocence hit me hard.

"Ah. Yes. I was expecting this to come." Breathing through the instant desire she invoked in me, I nodded in acknowledgment of her package. "Thank you."

"Oh. Okay. Um. If you don't mind..." Her fingers brushed against mine as she handed it over, and the simple contact seared me. So soft. So faint. Like the most decadent tickle. I resisted the thought of her hands on me as she immediately presented the electronic signature device with my receipt for the document.

As I scrawled my name on the screen, a whip cut through the air. The resounding smack on flesh was heightened with a woman's loud cry piercing through the music.

Becca flinched, jumping toward me. She was so startled by the sound that she bumped into a server, tipping drinks over. "Oh! I'm so sorry!"

I gestured for her to step aside, pleasantly surprised by how much easier she made this for me. "Here, let me help."

"No. That's okay." She brushed off her arm, as though her hand would remove all traces of dampness on her uniform sleeve. "I'll just go and—" Looking up and scanning her surroundings, she tried to find the exit.

People crowded around the scene being acted out, and she was quickly enraptured too. Absently brushing off her sleeve, she blinked and tried to avoid watching the man and woman fucking hard.

I stood there, triumphant in having this woman next to me. With her under my guard, she'd bring Murphy out of hiding. She had to.

But I couldn't whisk her away yet. I refused to jar her out of this secret fascination she couldn't break with the dirty, carnal sex scene yards away, live and rotten in technicolor.

"Oh..." Her lips parted open as she gaped at the man pushing his dick into the woman's pussy, sliding against the dildo already inside her. "Whoa..."

I refrained from smiling. *Holy fuck.*

Becca couldn't look away. She was in a lusty trance, staring at the couple, and I knew I had my answer about how innocent this woman was.

How enticingly sweet and clean—vanilla—she was to be so wowed by simple sex like this.

And it turned me on. It made her a target. I saw her as a dare. A challenge. The details blurred, rendering Becca not only a woman to hold hostage for a bigger purpose, but also as a new plaything to break and treasure.

If she could handle having her eyes opened wide to a hard fuck like that, I wanted to be the man to show her that world.

Stop.

She wasn't a member at this secret club. Becca wasn't here as a guest or looking for a good time.

She's a hostage.

Or she would be soon.

"This way," I encouraged her, gesturing for her to follow me.

"Oh!" She startled easily, blushing a wickedly sexy pink at being caught watching and admiring that scene. Off balance, likely turned on to the point that she was dripping, she staggered after me through the crowd. "Wait. I think I came in through a door over there."

I took her hand when a pair of men came close, eating her up with their predatory stares.

Fuck off. She's not yours.

She wasn't mine either, not like I instantly wanted her to be.

"This way," I repeated, thrilled when she held on tighter to my hand, nervous with those men eyeing her.

"Wait. I think—"

Too late.

Bringing her through another door that led to a private hallway, I held her slim body against mine and grabbed the bindings out of my pocket.

"Wait. What—I—" Her scream was cut off with the rope around her head, and I grinned in the darkness as I tied her up to be transported.

4

BECCA

I bucked and flung out my arms, wrestling as soon as the door closed behind us. This tall man guided me out of the throngs of people trying to get near that scene, but in the mix of confusion and the adrenaline rush of witnessing something so taboo, I was too flustered to think straight.

To realize this huge, strong man that staff member called Ivan was leading me further from the safety of others.

No one saw him steer me into this dark room. I was too hurried to understand where he was guiding me to resist or even react.

One moment, I was watching a man do wicked, naughty things to that woman, and now—

"Let me go!" My roar of a protest fell on his deaf ears, muffled into an incoherent blur of noise as he tightened the fabric around my head and cut off my scream.

My heart hammered against my ribs. I couldn't breathe fast enough through this panic overwhelming me to a dizzy state of almost passing out. All my senses felt fried as I tried to slow the blur of anxiety and terror to something I could manage and fight my way through.

His strong arms locked in a manacle around me as he lifted me.

Effortlessly. Carelessly, even. Up and away, he carried me with my mouth silenced behind a gag, my hands tied together. Still, I kicked and flung my legs the best I could to break free. In this darkness, I wouldn't know where to go, but if he lost his steely grip on me, I'd run. I would sprint away as fast as I could.

Because I'd had it.

This was *bullshit*.

A lifetime of men controlling me had me rabidly enraged, furious behind the stark horror and panic of what was happening.

Another man. *Another* asshole trying to decide my fate and take charge of me.

I was sick of it, so damn tired of being pushed around and used, moved as someone else saw fit. Doing what someone else deemed necessary. Years of repressed anger and frustration boiled to the surface, but with the uptick of ire, I couldn't breathe fast enough.

Dizzy and nauseated as Ivan hauled me through the darkness, I swallowed back the bile and willed my stomach to settle. If I puked while gagged, I'd choke. I could die. I could disappear, and that was not a possibility to leave Emily with. My baby needed me. I needed *her*, and this fucking asshole had another thing coming if he thought he could take me out of this nasty, depraved place and have his way with me.

Faint illumination broke through the darkness from the runner lines near the floor, and with the bobbing motion of being roughly carried away, I was more disoriented to the point I wanted to whimper.

No. I resisted the sound. I would be damned if I'd let this guy hear me vulnerable or scared.

Once more, for good measure, I bucked and squirmed to get free.

Nothing.

He had me in his hold, and he wasn't letting up at all.

What is he going to do? Force me into some weird scene and rape me in front of all those people in the club?

The second I entered the secretive building, I knew something was off. Never could I have anticipated that this was a sex club, but once I entered that bigger room and saw that it was, I wondered if I'd been set up.

Steven had asked me to get an envelope at a place like this. *Did he arrange this? What is going on!*

Worries and questions bombarded me as Ivan carried me through another door. When he dropped me into the backseat of a car, fear struck through my heart.

He was kidnapping me. While I was glad he wasn't going to subject me to something filthy and forbidden in the club against my will, I didn't like this outcome any better.

Why me?

Why?

I always knew my dad was crooked and that he wouldn't hesitate to use me for his corrupt plans.

Before him, Dom used me just the same, counting on me to be a connection to Steven for whatever illegal ideas they wanted to enact.

Now Ivan.

Kidnapped straight out of a sex club and rashly driven to an underground parking area.

Why me?

During the short ride, I let my fear and fury keep me alert. Ivan didn't drive for long. He spoke not a single word. Once he parked, he was quick to pull me out of the car. I didn't fight this time, biding my time and waiting for an opportune moment to strike out.

Seeing thugs and other criminal lackeys standing around warned me that I was outnumbered. I had to wait for a better moment to fight and run.

Upstairs, in what looked like an apartment, Ivan gave me a chance to rail and resist his handling.

He shoved me into a room, and I fell against a bed.

A bed. No different from what I saw at the sex club.

Maybe he did intend to have his way with me, just away from any spectators.

As I took a full look at him, registering how much taller he was now that it was just the two of us in the full light of the room, I shivered at how dark his eyes were. They burned with malice. With impatience. Yet, a sliver of intrigue glimmered there too as he watched me catch my breath and stagger to my feet.

Lifting his muscled hand, he showed how his tattoos showed beneath his collar and the end of his sleeve. Another hasty glance over his rugged face highlighted all the scars.

He was a hard man. Lived a hard life. And I didn't want any part of it.

He pushed my shoulder, rocking me back to the bed until I sat. Before more terror could fill me at the idea that he would rape me or worse, he flicked a knife open and brought it to my face.

I slammed my eyes shut, thinking of Emily. Keeping the image of my precious baby in mind, I tensed and braced for a lethal slice.

My life was over.

I'd never see her again.

Never watch her grow up.

Or maybe I would.

Ivan only pushed the blade down to remove the gag over my mouth. As the fabric fell, freeing the scraped skin there that was abused from the abrasion of the binding, I sucked in deeper inhales. Blinking my eyes open when I heard his step backward, retreating from me as he shoved his hands in his pockets, I tried to understand what was going on.

"Did you like what that man was doing to that woman at the club?" he asked, his voice gritty with lust and curiosity.

Of all things. Of *all* fucking things he could have asked me. I was suspended between utter fear and hot rage, stunned that he'd... that he'd *mock* me.

I gritted my teeth and lunged at him. "Let me go!"

He didn't break a sweat restraining me and setting me back on the bed. He waited until I sat up from the slump I fell into with my hands tied behind my back.

My chest heaving, my breath coming too shallow and fast as I fumed at him, I stared so hard that I prayed he'd see how angry I was.

A smirk. That was all he gave me. Not even breaking a sweat from handling me and forcing me to be submissive again.

"Did you?"

"No." I huffed, blowing my hair from my face. "What's it to you?" I sassed back. I wasn't going to assume he cared, that my reply mattered. He was in charge here. Not me.

"I noticed how intrigued you were."

I narrowed my eyes. "Intrigued? I wasn't intrigued. I was appalled. Shocked."

He arched one brow. "And aroused?"

"Fuck you!"

He sighed, not losing that dangerous aura but showing some modicum of patience.

"You're crazy. My reactions to that man and woman in that..."

"Scene. It's called a scene."

"I don't care what it's called. My opinions about that stuff don't matter. Let me go!"

He simply stared at me, almost as though he was content to wait me out and let me burn through this anger.

"You're crazy."

Still no reaction.

"I swear to God," I muttered hotly, fighting with my hands to see if I could slip through. "I swear, no man is ever going to control me again. I swear it."

"Who controls you?"

I glowered at him, wiggling my wrists to get out of this impossibly tight rope.

"Murphy?"

I went still, locking my arms.

"Steven Murphy," he clarified.

"Did he set you up to steal me out of that club? Huh? Did you set me up to go there?"

"I arranged for you to come to me," he admitted smugly. "But there is no way your father would ever work with the Valkov Bratva."

I was sure that name should have meant something to me, but I never involved myself with the names of the criminals my father was supposed to take down.

"How close are you to your father?"

I bit back a bitter bark of laughter, scowling as I looked away and scanned the meager contents of this room. "Not at all."

"You're not close with your father."

"Steven and I have never been close."

"But you seemed to think he'd set you up to go to that club."

I clenched my teeth, hating that I couldn't escape. "Because he asked me to go to a place like that and pick up something for him." I'd dropped off something tonight, through an ordered delivery with my job. Still, it bore enough similarities that I thought of Steven's last call to me.

"He asked me to help him. And I said no. I want nothing to do with places like that. With sex clubs and thugs and criminals like you. I've never agreed to do anything with Steven."

"Never."

I growled. The longer he stared at me with that cool authority, I was reminded that he was the boss here. Not me.

"What else has he asked you to do?"

"Favors. He never gave details, and I always shot him down before he'd tell me anything."

"You're his accomplice?" he asked.

"No." Once more, I fought the bindings on my wrists. "I have never worked with him, for him."

My answers didn't satisfy him. For a long time that I lost track of, Ivan peppered me with more questions about Steven. Relentlessly. Like a dog after a bone, he posed the same questions over and over as though he was waiting for me to slip.

Exhausted from fighting and the frustration of being captured because of my father, I hung my head and groaned. "Steven is secretive. I have never trusted him, and I don't ever plan to. He's a sperm donor, nothing more."

"What about the Rossini Family?"

I held my breath, staying rigid and still. *Why would he ask that?*

"Have you heard of the Rossinis, Becca?"

His tone changed from the direct, firm interrogative style like he was a journalist holding an interview. He asked me with mild amusement, and I knew he'd noticed my flinch at that name.

Shit.

"Becca…"

"No." I lifted my face defiantly, staring at him and hoping I could lie well enough that he wouldn't doubt my replies.

Of course, I'd heard of them. Dom Rossini was Emily's father, but I was too scared to reveal that fact.

He stared down at me. The silence of his careful study unnerved me, and I couldn't escape the feeling that I was caught in the crossfire somehow. That I was wedged in some kind of a twisted game between Mafia lords.

"You don't know anything about the Rossini Family?"

Pressing my lips together tighter, I vowed to shut the hell up and give nothing else away. All he'd get from me was the silent treatment. Nothing more, nothing less.

Still, he waited, crossing his arms and eyeing me so intensely, like he counted on me to break under his glare.

"Nothing to add?"

I bit the inside of my lower lip to remain as still as possible, keeping my gaze unwavering and locked on his.

You won't break me.

He smirked, taunting me to wonder what could make him lose that rein on this stare-down.

"I'll get my answers one way or the other."

Die trying, asshole.

"After all, every hostage has their purpose."

Turning to leave, he let me consider his parting words.

Hostage?

My heart raced even faster as the implications of his intentions sank in.

With all those questions about Steven. The thoughts that my father was hiding and being more secretive than ever, worrying about his "cover" so much that he'd asked me to handle a favor for him.

He had to be staying down low for a reason, and Ivan wanted to hold me captive to lure him out.

A pawn. I was taken to be a pawn, but the joke was on him.

Steven didn't care about me. Only himself.

The man who fathered me didn't care whether I lived or died.

I stared at the door, zoning out as worry flooded me all over again, and I wondered when Ivan would realize the same thing—how dispensable I really was.

5

IVAN

Becca didn't tell me anything. The sight of her tight-lipped, stubborn, and angry with her sizzling green gaze on me like that...

I paced in the hallway outside the room I'd locked her in. Back and forth, I walked out this instant lust that she'd lit within me.

My dick ached, straining under my pants. I breathed fast, riled up with desire and a potent hit of needing to fuck that defiant woman hard and fast.

To make her bend.

To make her talk.

I wasn't bluffing. I *would* get my answers out of her. I wouldn't fail. But I had to step back, away where I could inhale and not notice her fresh, innocent scent. Apart from her so I wouldn't be drawn further under the spell to want her so badly.

Her pushing back was my kryptonite. Her tough exterior and pretending to be ballsy with a silent treatment and cold shoulder made me want her more.

I would get my answers.

She was a hostage, and she had a purpose here.

That purpose wasn't for my pleasure. She wasn't a subbie looking for a firm lover. She wasn't a guest at any of the clubs, seeking a good time.

She was a hostage, to be kept as a bait that should make Murphy reveal himself. And then I could take him down.

Heaving out a final deep breath, I glowered at the closed door. Behind that wooden panel was my enemy's daughter, an innocent woman who wouldn't ever understand the depth of my desire, the darkness of my kinks. Becca was bound in there not for a good fuck, but to serve as a way of pulling her father out of hiding.

Or will she?

I compared the little that she did share. At first, she was too sassy for her own good, responding to my questions about Murphy. She didn't fill me with hope, though. By her account, Steven Murphy was not close with his daughter, perhaps so distant and aloof that the man might not care about her being held here.

Fuck. I rubbed my hand over the back of my neck, worrying that Becca might not deliver a purpose at all.

When I asked about the Rossinis, though, she'd barely had the time to hide her reaction. She knew them, or something about them. She had to if the mere mention of the Rossinis got her flinching, her eyes widening more with fear.

If Murphy was working with the Rossinis, she had to know something about either party, and whatever nugget of information she could expose, I'd take it. I had to find that fucker one way or another.

Adjusting the bulge of my erection, I smoothed down my shirt and tamped back this instant flare of lust.

This wasn't the time for that.

No kinks. No fantasies. She was a hostage and not for me to enjoy.

I reentered the room, pleased to see that she hadn't moved in the few minutes I'd stepped into the hallway for a breather.

She put up a good fight, reacting to the fight-or-flight instinct when I removed her from the club. I dismissed all her attempts to squeeze her hands out. She wasn't slipping out of that rope. This was far from my first rodeo of tying someone up.

Becca hadn't taken this experience easily, restraining and wrestling to get free.

Yet she wasn't so stupid to assume she could launch at me or attack in here to get her way.

Sitting on the bed, staring at me mulishly like that, she appeared to be a recalcitrant woman who needed a good spanking. An attitude adjustment. Someone to steer her into more obedience.

Dammit. My dick stirred again, hardening as I matched her stern gaze.

She wasn't backing down. I bet she intended to sit there silently and try to wait me out.

But why? Why fight me so hard? Besides the obvious consequences of being taken hostage, why be *this* stubborn to fight me with answers?

More questions filled my mind as I struggled to resist the allure of her.

Is she a spy?

She admitted that Murphy previously asked her to do a "favor" for him at a sex club. That told me she was familiar with his proclivity to do shady shit. How much more was she aware of?

Is she working with him and acting like Murphy is no friend or ally of hers?

I wanted to believe her when she insisted that she wasn't close with Murphy. Failing to miss her immediate reaction to my mention of the Rossini name had to mean something more.

Are they all working together? If I knew what Murphy planned with the Rossinis, I could use that scheme against them and bring them all down.

What the fuck are you up to? I narrowed my eyes at her, desperate to root out something useful from behind her closed lips. It felt like I was reaching at any doubt and guess as an excuse to resist her. No matter how long I appreciated her bold stare, I realized I wasn't infallible.

Becca called to me on a cellular level, and I decided to ride with it.

"Anything else you'd like to say?" I asked, stepping closer as I pulled a long length of a silky sash from my pocket.

She swallowed as she watched what I showed her in my hands as I stalked forward.

No? She remained quiet.

"Still gonna play this game and act like you can't speak up?"

I set my knee on the edge of the bed, right between her legs. Coming this close, I forced her to lean back as I reached for the headboard. One slip of the sash around the metal bars was enough, because I was sure she'd be fighting to get closer to me, not away, once I amped up my efforts here.

"Silent treatment?" I goaded as I gripped her collar and yanked down. Buttons flew off, and she gasped at the destruction of her uniform shirt. Beneath the pale lavender fabric, a black lacy camisole stretched over her chest, her breasts testing the endurance of the material as she breathed hard and fast.

"That's all you got for me?" I reached behind her, rubbing my side against her tits as I sliced through the ropes at her wrist to retie her hands over her head. The silky bindings looked fucking perfect on her. The contrast of the dark red satin against her pale skin...

Gorgeous. As was the panic in her eyes as I shoved her backward until the binding on the headboard tugged her to lie back.

"Silence?" I raised my brows as she shivered, staring at me with fear in her blue eyes wide with alarm.

Still, she kept her mouth shut.

I flipped my knife around and traced the butt of the handle along her lips. Rubbing back and forth again, I taunted her to part those lips and answer me.

"We'll see about that."

After pushing her legs down, I curled my fingers around the hem of her shorts and pulled. Once, twice. I forced the garment down, along with her panties.

"Nothing to say yet?" I watched her, reinvigorated and so fucking revved up with lust coursing through my veins.

Stubborn as fuck. Strong to a fault. As I dragged her clothes off her, leaving her shorts and panties at one ankle before I tied them to other posts at the foot of the bed, I waited for her to break.

To speak up. To tell me to wait. To stop what I was doing.

It was a game, a battle of wills, and as I checked that all four limbs were secure, I wondered if she was silent because she had nothing to say or if she was insistent on keeping her information from me.

"Not gonna tell me to stop?" I teased.

I knelt on the bed, feasting my eyes on her creamy skin. So smooth, so soft. All for my pleasure if I so wanted.

Keeping my eyes on hers, steadying my breath as my cock strained beneath my zipper, I slid the handle of my knife up along the inside of her thigh. She trembled and shook, so overwhelmed that she closed her eyes tight.

Back and forth. Up and down. I traced the blade of my knife over her flesh without marring her once. Then I repeated it with the thick cylinder of the handle.

At her pussy, I pushed and rubbed her, grinding the rounded head of the handle at her entrance.

Glistening and plump, pink and succulent, her cunt captured my attention. She was wet. Aroused. And I grinned as I watched her squeeze her eyes shut tighter.

A sweet whimper left her lips, but she clamped them into a thin line once more.

"What do you have to tell me, Becca?" I crooned as I wedged the tip of my knife handle into her pussy.

She panted, breathing faster as I penetrated her. With my hand wrapped in the last of the silky binding I hadn't needed to use on her, I gripped the blade and worked the handle in deeper.

Fuck. Yes.

She was so tight. Dripping wet. Her tits rose and fell faster with shallow inhales, and I fought the urge to rip her shirt down so I could see the nipples that beaded beneath the thin, stretchy fabric.

"Want to come clean and tell me what you're up to with your dad?" I pushed the handle in deeper, gritting my teeth at how she bucked her hips up, sucking it in.

"You like that, huh?"

She shook her head, lying as she arched into my touch.

"If you tell me…" I pulled the knife out, and back. Again and again, I fucked her little pussy with my weapon. "Then I'll keep going."

"I—" She cinched her eyes shut tighter yet, straining with a grimace of need and frustration.

"You what, Becca?" I pushed faster, deeper, rubbing and dragging the ribbed hilt over the tender, tight walls of her cunt.

Frantic, she shook her head. She didn't stop lifting up to meet me. Her heels pushed into the mattress for better purchase. The muscles in her arms flexed and tensed as she tried to hold on to the bindings at her wrists. With her whole body, she lied, rushing closer to get off on my knife handle sliding in and out of her cunt.

"What is it? What do you *really* want to tell me?"

An incoherent reply was all she uttered. Maybe it was a grunt. Recognizing the signs of her being so close to coming, feeling her pussy starting to near an orgasm, I stopped.

Abruptly. I withdrew the knife and retreated to stand on the bed.

A keening cry slipped from her. She bucked, her stomach tensing as she thrust into the air as though she followed my shadow.

"No."

I watched her protest, eyes cloudy with desire and impatience. Frustration too. She stared up at me, her breaths labored. Scowling, she kept a close watch as I lifted my knife and licked the hilt, tasting her tangy cream.

"You fucking asshole."

"Gonna talk now?"

She growled, flailing at her bindings. When she stuck with growls and grunts, clenched teeth and sneers, I shrugged.

"I refuse to play games with you!"

I ignored her wrath, walking around the bed and willing my erection to give up on her. This *was* a game. And I would be the winner.

A swift slice through the ties at her ankles had her halfway freed.

Then another cut through the tie to the headboard lowered her trembling arms. Whether she shook from fear, anger, or disappointment at having her orgasm withheld, I didn't know.

But I'd let her stew on it.

Leaving her again, I ignored the sounds of her protests and fury. I slammed the door, locking it as I dropped my brow to the wood. Breathing hard, I struggled to regain my composure.

She was too sexy. Too inviting, a challenge I didn't want to quit on. *Fuck, does she get to me.*

But this was a game. A ploy. I had to remember that.

Becca was a hostage. A means to an end. And I hated that she got under my skin so much, turned me on so quickly that I was starting to lose sight of that.

As I calmed down, waiting to erase the image of her spread out on that bed, sucking my knife into her cunt and making me wish it were my dick, I lost sight of that.

I couldn't afford to go weak around her.

Walking away, I vowed not to.

I'd be damned if a sweet innocent like her—a hostage and pawn in this feud—could threaten my determination to find and kill her father.

6

BECCA

Ivan slammed the door and locked it. The *click* reached my ears like a final sound, almost as though it was the last word of that interaction. He was in charge. I couldn't mistake the dynamic going on here.

What I couldn't understand was why he'd slashed through the ties keeping me in place. He wanted to keep me captive, that much was obvious. No windows gave me a chance to escape here. Nothing for a weapon to defend myself should he come back, as if I could survive attacking him or getting physical.

My hands shook as I scrambled off the bed and hurried to fetch my shorts and panties. Little good they would do me now. Since he'd... he'd...

Oh, God. I couldn't even go there. The thought of him using a knife, the hard handle like that to tease me and insert it into where I'd gotten so wet and slippery with arousal...

A sob rose up my throat, but I swallowed it down. If he could hear me through that door, I didn't want to give him the satisfaction of knowing I was reacting to what he did.

He'd put me on the spot because I'd gone silent and uncooperative on him. He'd played that nasty, wicked game with me, taunting me with an object like that in such a filthy way, all to get me to talk.

What did he want? I told him that I didn't associate with Steven. I didn't know anything about the Rossinis other than what a lying, manipulative asshole Dominic Rossini was as he led me on to think I was worth something, that my art was valuable enough to be sponsored.

Yet he had to go so far as to violate me and make me feel so...

No. Stop. He wasn't getting anything from me. Not the submission he wanted, not like that, dammit.

Tears stung my eyes as I shoved my legs through my clothes roughly and quickly, wishing for more and more layers to hide behind. Tempted to grab the blanket and wrap it around me like a shield, I paced in the room. Hugging myself didn't make an impact. As long as I was here, strips of fabric still tied around my wrists, behind this locked door, I was stuck and not going anywhere until he thought I was no longer useful as a hostage or a pawn in whatever vendetta he had against Steven.

Tense and confused, not to mention strained from coming so close to coming in the most unexpected and forbidden way possible, I paced and worried, fretted and freaked out, slowly and silently.

What was going to happen? What would he do with me? Was he here because of my father's plans? Because I was the mother of a Rossini baby?

Before I could let the unanswered questions flood me and overwhelm me to the point of anxious hysteria, the lock on the door clicked.

I spun, facing the door as it was pushed open. My heart raced, lodged in my throat. My lungs strained to bring in air fast enough. The immediate spike of fear that pierced through me dizzied me, but all I could do was lean one hand on the bed. Keeping the bed between myself and the door, I tensed and waited.

Ivan didn't come alone. Another rugged man accompanied him, and at the first glance, I noticed the familial resemblance. A brother? Cousin? Whoever he was, he looked just as dangerous as Ivan, muscled and packing a gun, a cold, stern, glowering expression with cautious eyes.

He checked me out, a blunt once-over like he was assessing me as a threat or a risk to handle efficiently. His regard didn't intimidate me like Ivan's did. This newcomer didn't eye me with blunt interest like Ivan had. Ivan once again roved his smoldering stare up and down me, his lips kicked up on one side like he was amused. Humored.

Is he thinking about what he did to me?

Is he imagining what I looked like?

Is he—

I stood up straighter, determined to stay strong, both against him and his buddy and my own stupid thoughts. It hardly mattered what he thought. His opinions couldn't matter. What he'd done was wrong. Tying me up. Removing my clothes. Sticking... anything inside me like that.

Humiliation mixed with awful regret, but I realized it was a conscious action to get so wet and turned on, eager to come then. My body betrayed me. My pussy ached, and I was a puppet to the magic of desire.

Still, I hated that he'd been able to play me like that, fine-tuned toward how to get me to surrender so quickly.

Ivan wasn't a man to trust, not at all. So I made sure to watch him closer than this other man. I vowed to never lower my guard again, even if hope was futile with him in charge and dominating the situation.

"Where is it?" the other man asked. He lifted his hand to me, and I furrowed my brow. I didn't have a clue what he thought I might have on me.

"I took it when I transported her." Ivan held out my phone. At the sight of the old-model device, I clenched my teeth. Seeing it in his hands proved that I wouldn't have a chance to call for help, but even if I could, I didn't know who to call. 911 was an obvious option, but with Steven affiliated and employed by the NYPD, I couldn't chance the dispatcher somehow getting him involved. If Ivan was so determined to find out intel about Steven, I bet the man coming here wouldn't be good.

"The passcode." The other man accepted the phone and paired his firm request with an arched brow of expectation.

I swallowed.

"She's been giving me the silent treatment, Dmitri," Ivan dryly stated, as though I was a troublesome child due for a scolding.

"The passcode," Dmitri repeated.

I zoned out, staring at my phone. I didn't give a shit what they wanted to look at on there. I had nothing to hide.

Except Emily.

Pictures were saved in a folder that I used to download onto my laptop. I took far too many of them when the device's battery was sufficient. It was such an old phone that I never had enough space to save many images. The ones that I had on there were no doubt all of the adorably chunky baby I so adored.

I couldn't risk them finding her. I had to protect her at all costs, and if this whole thing had something to do with the Rossini Family, I had to take every precaution to keep my baby from them.

Dmitri sighed, glancing at Ivan.

He looked at me nonplussed as he tilted his head to the side. "What are you hiding?"

I shook my head. This was hurting my head. Frustration gave way to exhaustion. "Nothing. I'm not hiding anything."

Dmitri raised his brows, still waiting.

"I told you, I do not get involved with Steven's plans and schemes."

"The passcode," Ivan ordered. His tone was just as bossy and demanding as Dmitri's was, but the glint of a challenge in his eyes, as though he looked forward to my being difficult again, tormented me.

"Five, two, nine, nine." I exhaled a long breath with that forfeit.

Dmitri tapped on the screen, then he brought another object up close, likely interfering with what I had on there. Not knowing was agony. "What are you doing?" I hated how weak and nervous my voice was.

"Tracking your call history," Dmitri answered, surprising me. I hadn't actually counted on them to reply.

"What... what else?" I swallowed hard. My throat was so damn dry.

"What are you so nervous about?"

Emily. My baby. Please, don't. I pressed my lips together and struggled to think of what to say that wouldn't piss him off. Surely, he couldn't care if I had a child.

Once the worry deepened, I wondered if that was it. If Emily, my baby, was the key to what was going on. All this time he'd been messing with me and playing with me like a toy held hostage, I'd been stuck with the assumption that Steven was bluffing. That Dom might actually be interested in custody like Steven told me.

A deep sense of panic threaded through my mind, and I became frantic to figure it out.

"Previous calls to Dominic Rossini." Dmitri held the phone up to show Ivan. "Going back as far as a year ago."

Ivan crossed his arms. "What's that about?"

"What, what do you mean?" Even though my voice shook, I kept my chin raised, my head held up high. I wasn't about to offer information. If they wanted to know something specific about things not to do with me or Emily, I didn't want to be in that discussion at all. The less I knew, the better. Ignorance, especially with anything Steven or these crime lords did, was preferred.

"I won't bother with a step backward of asking *if* you know him. What's your relation to Dom Rossini?"

His withering stare challenged me to tell the truth, but I couldn't. Not yet. Not until I knew why he cared.

"I'm not related to him."

"What is your connection to him?" Dmitri asked.

"He..." I licked my lips, under pressure and not knowing what to say.

"He what?" Ivan lowered his arms and narrowed his eyes at me, becoming even more threatening with just those movements.

"He was a potential sponsor for my artwork." Skimming over the truth seemed like the best option, and I prayed that it would work.

"Your artwork?" Dmitri asked, skeptical. He glanced at Ivan as though to silently ask *are you hearing this right?*

"You're an artist?" Ivan lifted his chin, looking down his nose at me.

I nodded. "Dom was supposed to help me get my feet in the door. The art world is a highly competitive one, and he had connections in Europe, with galleries and commission project heads."

Dmitri returned to my phone, scrolling and snooping.

"He took me to Italy, mostly," I added, nervous whether Ivan would believe this truth. "My paintings didn't do well anywhere, but I did garner some interest for my sculptures." I felt so silly, insignificant. Talking about my passion, about a creative endeavor like this with a man who couldn't care about anything like it. Thugs and criminals didn't waste time with masterpieces that only existed for the purpose of beauty and provoking thoughts.

"I don't believe you." Ivan shook his head, tilting his head to the side to see what Dmitri showed him on the screen.

"It looks more like you were dating him, according to these texts." Dmitri glanced up at me, wearing the same expression of doubt Ivan did.

"No. I..."

"You deny it?" Ivan asked.

"I... No. I supposed he was dating me. But it wasn't real. It was..." I hung my head for a moment, hating that I had to relive this pain. "He was using me. Just to keep tabs on my father. He knew I was Steven's daughter and he wanted to stay abreast of his actions." I shrugged, wincing at the tension on my muscles after being tied up. "That's all men do." I glared at Ivan, emphasizing that he fit in that category too. "Men see me as a prop, a tool to get what they want. Steven has always seen me as a person to use and manipulate, but I never gave him the chance."

That was a partial lie. I suspected something might be fishy from the beginning when Steven introduced me to Dom. But I'd been so excited for a sponsor and finding a wealthy person who seemed to care about my art that I got suckered in.

"I am not and never have been involved with anything Steven does. Dom either."

My phone rang, buzzing in Dmitri's hand. Both men looked at me, and I tensed.

It had to be Hannah. She had to be so worried that I hadn't come home from work yet. She'd been with Emily all this time.

"Interesting," Dmitri said. "This number seems familiar."

What? That wasn't interesting. It was odd. It wasn't Hannah, then.

He glared at me. "Answer it." Then he pressed the *accept call* button and lifted it on speaker.

"Hello?"

"Becca." A man I didn't recognize spoke. "I'm calling from the Rossini offices."

Dread coiled in my stomach. It had to be someone from Dom, reaching about custody, just like Steven had warned.

He cleared his throat. "Where is Emily, Becca?"

My pulse tripled. I blinked, unbalanced and weak with that one taunting question.

Emily.

The call was dropped. A beep sounded, signaling the disconnection.

My knees gave way as I dropped to the floor.

Emily!

She should have been safe with Hannah at home. She was supposed to be fine despite her father's identity. All I ever wanted was to raise her with the love I never had myself as a child.

But I didn't know where she was. I wasn't home to see her and protect her.

I was here, caught in some twisted, confusing mess that couldn't matter to me or her.

Terror streaked through me, chilling me from the inside out.

If that man knew to ask about my baby, Dom knew that she existed.

If that man knew to call me directly and ask about where she was… it implied he had a reason to assume she was missing, just like I was.

7

IVAN

Becca lowered her head, hiding behind her hands as she cried. No noises left her, but there was no missing how worked up she was. Her shoulders shook. Her long, red, wavy curls hung low, curtaining her face. Crouched over on the floor, she looked broken and wretched with the end of that call.

From a Rossini.

Dmitri caught my attention, gesturing toward the closed door behind us. I nodded, frowning at Becca breaking down on the floor. Staying in here with her would have left us with two options. Ignore her distress and demand answers or try to calm her down so she could speak clearly again. Neither of those appealed, so it wasn't hard to leave her be, to give her a chance to collect herself as I stepped out with my brother.

Dmitri closed the door, but I reached over to lock it. She seemed upset, but for all I knew, it could be an act. She could be faking it and planning to use her tears and mood as a distraction to slip away.

With all the guards around my building, she wouldn't get far. But I didn't want to take any chances.

"I'm not sure that number came from a Rossini source," Dmitri said, still holding her phone.

"You said it was interesting."

"Yeah. As a burner that's come up before. But we can't place it."

I shook my head at him. "He identified as a Rossini."

Dmitri huffed. "So? Anyone could claim to be someone else on the phone. She didn't seem to recognize the voice."

I appreciated his insight. Everything that Becca did, everything she said, I took it with a heavy sense of doubt. I wanted to assume she was the enemy. I had to view her as a liar I couldn't believe or trust. I was second-guessing every moment together. Because I wanted her so viscerally, because she seemed to burrow in deep and capture me in a way not many women could, I was desperate for a solid reason for why I had to forget about anything happening. I needed her to be "bad" or to be the enemy to prevent myself from letting it get into my head that I could enjoy her.

I didn't think I'd ever wanted a woman so quickly and badly as I did her. I couldn't explain it, and I didn't want to.

Hearing my brother's assessment gave me much-needed guidance. If he seemed to think she wasn't acting, maybe I was overthinking it all and searching for excuses to pin her as my foe.

"No Rossini seems to be looking for her." Dmitri set her phone on a table, leaving the tracking ware attached to it. "We've already put it out there that Becca's been taken. Not confirming nor denying that *we* have her under Valkov custody, just that she's been taken."

"And?"

"And nothing." He shook his head. "The Rossinis aren't reacting to this news that Becca's captured. Murphy isn't either. He hasn't returned any calls that we've set up with informants and moles that he might listen to."

So... no one cares? That made no sense. She was his flesh and blood. Murphy had to care to some degree. He cared enough to stay in contact with her and lean on her to do favors that she always rejected.

"Something's not adding up," I replied.

"I agree, but we'll have to wait and see what happens." Dmitri glanced at the time. "It's early yet."

I nodded. It was. I'd only snatched her from that club a few hours ago.

The whole purpose of holding Becca hostage was to lure Murphy out long enough so I could kill him. That didn't mean that everything would happen quickly. The fucker might be biding his time and trying to see how he could play this.

"Did she say anything else?" Dmitri asked, seeming ready to leave.

"No." I gripped the back of my neck and blew out a long breath. "Silent treatment and being uncooperative."

He grinned. "Oh, like that'd stop you." As he went to leave, accomplishing what he'd come for—setting her phone to be tracked—he was done. "Like you can't get someone to talk."

I wondered how far I'd have to push her to speak up. In protest as I fucked her. In agreement and begging me to fuck her.

No! I had to stop seeing her as a sweet cunt to bury myself in. This attraction was a problem, but I'd use it to my advantage.

I hesitated before going back to her room. Something just wasn't making sense about all of this, and I refused to think with my cock or let my darkness take over. I had to be smart about this. If something seemed off, niggling at me, it had to mean something *was* off.

Are things not going smoothly between Murphy and the Rossinis then? If trouble was brewing between the crooked cop and one of the Italian Mafia lords, I could probably use that antagonism to my advantage and benefit from the trouble. Maybe that was how I could get Murphy to reveal himself.

In the meantime, though...

I faced the door and stalked toward it.

I wouldn't let a minute go to waste with Becca. Dmitri was right. I could get anyone to talk. Silent treatments didn't last with me. And she was about to learn that lesson.

She whirled around to face me, her face clear of tears but a scowl of petulance and anxiousness.

"Who is Emily?" I asked as I unbuttoned my shirt.

She opened and closed her mouth, startled with how quickly I demanded an answer for that. Her gaze dropped to my chest—scarred and tatted—as I revealed it quickly.

"I don't..." She backed up as I stalked toward her. "I—"

I grabbed her arms and turned her just as I finished getting my shirt off. Using it to twine her hands together, I secured her to the bedframe once more. Still standing, she stumbled to stay upright.

"Wait. No. I—"

"You tell me who Emily is, and I'll consider stopping." I did the opposite, tearing her shorts and panties off her again. The faint twinge of the scent of her cream remained in the air, and I dragged in a deep breath as I kicked her feet to widen her stance.

"No. Ivan, please."

I was done torturing myself with waiting. I wrenched her camisole up, and it split at the seams, revealing her back to me. All that smooth skin arched back as I reached between us and thrust my fingers into her pussy.

With how fast I'd come upon her, she wasn't soaked—yet. But it wasn't a rough slide in. Slick already, she sucked me in. Her head jerked back with a loud groan of surprise and desire.

"Who is Emily? Tell me." I pistoned my fingers into her fast, punishing her for being so difficult. As she pushed back to me, I pushed my arm around her and took hold of her tit. Squeezing hard, I pinched the hard tip of her nipple.

Her loud cry was sweet music. And her pussy dripped more, coating my fingers as I hammered my digits into her with punishing speed.

"What are you hiding?"

She shook her head, wordlessly denying me any information.

"Where is Murphy hiding?"

Still, she shook her head, gasping at my brutal fingering as I dropped my pants and kicked them off.

"Nothing? You still won't fucking talk?" I gritted my teeth, lifting her until I could slam my dick deep inside her. In one swift punch into her slippery entrance, I seated myself in her tightness.

Oh, fuck.

I closed my eyes, relishing this perfect squeeze for a moment and staying still to let the sensations of being gloved by her tightness wash over me.

"Ivan..." She struggled to catch her breath, teasing me with that husky moan of my name.

I dug my fingers into her breast, reveling in the exquisite feel of her everywhere. In front of me, wrapped around my dick, and filling my hand.

It wasn't enough. I strained to wait and let her understand that I was in charge.

"Nothing to say?" I rasped, burning with the need to pound into her.

Her hair brushed against my face as she shook it no and canted her ass toward me.

I held her tight and pummeled her wet cunt. Over and over, thrusting so hard the headboard hit the wall. I had no toys. Only her hands were bound. But it would have to do.

"Tell me," I demanded.

As she trembled, sweat dripping between us in a slick layer as our skin slapped together and rubbed hard, she whined. "I don't. I don't know anything!"

It was possible. And improbable. I wasn't buying it that she was ignorant and unaware of something I could use to smoke Murphy out of wherever he was hiding.

What became crystal clear and undeniable was how much she wanted this. Hard. Fast. Urgent and brutal. Her pussy welcomed me in, pulling me in deep as she pushed her sweet ass against me and tried to meet me thrust for thrust.

She was caving, no longer protesting but rushing to come for me.

"Fuck." I stepped forward, lifting my foot to the bed and forcing her head down. At this angle, I could pound into her harder and quicker, driving her body forward without stop. Shoving upward, I hit her just right, so deep in her pussy that she cried out louder.

Clutching her thigh, I wrapped her leg up and out of my way to spread her wide open. Her hair glistened and shone, golden among the auburn as the tresses shook and swung. I couldn't see it, but one reach down confirmed her generous tits swayed and jiggled violently.

All she could do was hang her head down toward her bound arms and take it. And she did. She took every gritty, greedy bit of this hard fuck, moaning like a sex goddess and feeding my need to explode and soak her womb with my hot cum.

When I did, it was with her long-awaited orgasm. Her pussy walls clenched my cock, milking me with her swollen tissue as I jerked up with a final hard rock of my hips against her ass.

I didn't get any intel, but knowing I'd fucked her brains out and made her come felt like a decent consolation prize of a reward.

Straining to breathe faster, I leaned back and wiped my hand over my brow, smearing the sweat collecting there to fall to the side. One shove of her ass had her falling forward onto the bed.

Limp and lax, she was clumsy as I slipped out of her. I stood, watching her bare body as she shivered and shook, coming down from the rush of coming so violently with me.

Sinking to the mattress, she ended up twisting her arms, rolling another kink in my shirt that kept her tied up.

I couldn't take my eyes off her. All this sweet innocence that I'd taken.

She landed on her back. Eyes closed. Mouth open as she panted. Flush and thoroughly fucked. Gorgeous.

I furrowed my brow, blinking as I caught my breath yet.

That line…

I focused on the scar low on her abdomen.

A marking of a C-section.

Becca wasn't just the daughter of my enemy. She was a mother. She'd had a child.

I couldn't stop the hunch that rapidly formed. The way she'd tucked in and fell when that caller asked where Emily was told me enough. She'd crumpled to the floor like someone had wrenched her heart out. Like her body couldn't remain strong enough against a chance of Emily being missing.

I gripped her ankle and tugged. It did the trick. She flinched in surprise and opened her eyes to gawk at me.

"Is Emily your child?"

8

BECCA

Thoughts couldn't form fast enough. After Ivan's direct question, flat-out inquiring whether Emily was my child, all I could do was stare at him in shock. And breathe. My lungs didn't seem capable of holding much air for long, and I wondered if he'd fucked me so hard that he'd driven my lungs up into a mess in my ribcage.

Weak and startled by the force of that orgasm, I felt blindsided as I sank into the softness of the bed. Blood drained down my arms, numbing my limbs with my hands still tied over my head. Spinning as I fell hadn't helped. I'd torqued another twist into the binding. I felt every tight cinch of it, and I worried I'd cut off my circulation.

Ivan didn't miss my wince and subtle tug on the knots. He stood there, naked and catching his breath too. Every glorious inch of his rugged, chiseled body was there to look at, and I struggled not to stare and get lost in how ripped and big he was.

As he stepped closer, his dick hard and glistening with our combined cum, he reached up for the knots and loosened them.

Wait. Was he tying me up strictly to keep me captive or for some kinky level of pleasure he preferred, fucking women who were bound up? Bondage. I was lacking a varied sex life, but I'd read romance books. I saw movies. I knew what the term was, but I'd never considered that I would ever be a participant in it.

Or that I'd like it so much.

Lying here bare and shivering from the force of coming so hard and quickly, I felt vulnerable and exposed. Inside and out. Those intense stares Ivan bestowed on me were piercing, cutting through me like he was looking at my soul and finding me suspicious.

When would I learn? I hated the realization that he'd gotten me so easily, so fast. I hadn't done anything to deserve or encourage this situation. I'd only been doing my job, set up to go to that club and even meet this rough man.

But my body... My tender entrance was so sticky with copious juices. I'd *wanted* it. He hadn't asked. He'd forced it, but the second I felt his big, hot body bracing behind mine, I was aroused.

I'd wanted him to take me, and when he hadn't held back, brutal and impatient, I felt... alive.

Not used. Not violated. Unlike when Dom impregnated me with Emily, with Ivan, I had the impression that I was coveted, treasured, even if he'd shown it in a gritty, raw method.

I was betrayed, my body showing me how I stupidly wanted all the gruffness Ivan could give me, but it was different. With Dom, it was worse. He'd spent all that time in psychological warfare, leading me on and tricking me to think that I'd mattered. He was cunning, playing on my goals for my artwork.

Ivan was direct, blunt and taking what he wanted, but also giving me what I hadn't realized I'd needed. He somehow understood what I wanted and delivered, seeing to my pleasure and expediting a shattering orgasm that should have had me curling up to pass out by now.

I didn't experience that sickening awareness that I'd been abused. Not like when Dom raped me so awfully and with disdain and scorn.

All I felt was a renewal of energy. Of feeling so alive and invigorated.

And worried.

"Becca." He lowered my ankle, having my attention. "Is Emily your child?" He repeated it with less of that shocked tone, implying he had a hunch about it and was confident that he was right.

I sat up and lowered my arm, shaking it as the blood flowed through freer. My skin tingled, and I winced as I formulated a response. That silent treatment stuff wasn't working. All my fight to be firm against him seemed unwise now.

He surprised me, picking up my wrist and rubbing the sore skin there. I hadn't expected aftercare, any affection at all, and I refused to let it disarm me. He could be playing a solo show of good-cop-bad-cop, being brutish and violent to fuck me then deceptively kind and tender afterward.

His callused, rough fingers on my flesh felt too good to reject, though, and I sighed as I looked him in the eye.

"Emily is my daughter."

I almost counted on him to react smugly, some kind of an *a-ha* moment of breaking me down to finally reply. The other questions he'd asked weren't going to produce new information. He could flog me with inquiries about Steven and I still wouldn't have anything to tell him. He could pepper me with more about the Rossinis, and my replies would remain limited. Before he'd fucked me, when Dmitri stopped in too, they'd played a stupid scenario of beating this interrogation to death, asking the same things over and over.

I knew nothing. But this new question about Emily, I could be honest about that.

"She's my ten-month-old baby, currently with a sitter who's likely worried to death that I'm not home yet."

He narrowed his eyes, switching to massage my other wrist. "Is that an attempt to persuade me into letting you go?"

I rolled my eyes. "You've made it clear who's in charge here."

"Then don't be surprised when I expect you to tell me what you're doing with the Rossinis. Why one called you about your daughter."

I shook my head, sighing and so damn tired of the ups and downs of this hellish night.

"I don't know what any Rossini would want with me. I don't associate with Steven. I don't associate with any of the people he allies with or tries to arrest and kill. I've never been a part of that world. My only fault is sharing DNA with one of New York's most crooked cops.

"I can't tell if the Rossinis *do* want anything to do with me. I can't tell if it's all a bluff. I assume half of what I am told is a lie. That habit started with Steven."

He released my hand and crossed his arms, staring down at me as he listened.

I fought not to glance at his dick, tempted, but too sobered on this topic. After a deep breath, I explained more. "Dominic Rossini is Emily's father. He ended his 'relationship' with me after I conceived her, and I don't think he ever knew I had a baby. That Emily is his."

He smirked. "That call suggests otherwise."

I scowled. "Not really. Come on. Someone calling and saying they *are* a Rossini? Who answers like that or identifies themselves like that?"

"How did you meet Dom?"

"Steven. Through my interest in art. When I first met him, I thought they had to be friends, and when Dom learned that I was an artist, he took a natural interest in me as a fellow lover of the fine arts. It wasn't until later that he'd only strung me along to keep an eye on Steven through me. To always stay in the loop."

"For what?"

I shrugged. "Something I didn't know about and didn't want anything to do with. I have lived my whole life hearing about or seeing Steven associating with criminal scum. All kinds of seedy people. I learned early on to look away and cover my ears. That's not the life I've ever wanted to live."

"You want me to believe you don't know what Murphy and Rossini were working on together?"

"I don't even know if they *were* working together. It was something like a friend of a friend scenario, and I was so gullible to think that Dom wanted to genuinely sponsor my artwork that I stuck around and hung with him in Italy. Whereas, he saw me as a pawn. A tool. Something to tie him to Steven. It's always lies and bluffs. No trust."

His guarded expression suggested he viewed me the same. Not

trusting me. At least he'd already been honest about his intentions—
the part about keeping me as a hostage. I couldn't equate his blunt-
ness about why he'd taken me captive with any other sentiment of
trust or faith, though. Now that he knew about Emily, I felt
cornered.

Some of that panic swept back in, chasing away the glow of an
intensely satisfying orgasm.

"Please." I licked my lips and begged him with a direct stare.
"Please, don't hurt her."

His brows dipped down as he considered me. "Hurt *her*?"

"Emily."

"What about hurting you?"

I parted my mouth but realized the naughty retort that first came
to mind wouldn't be helpful.

*Hurt me... like you did driving your dick in like that? Hurt me as in
surprising me and taking me without any warning?*

"What?" He lowered to grab his pants. "What was that look for?"

It was ridiculous, but a blush warmed my cheeks. "I, uh, I didn't
mind that pain." I feebly lifted my hands to show the redness on my
wrists before placing them over my lap and hiding my bare pussy that
still felt so sticky and sore.

He grunted as he pulled his pants on. Maybe it was a laugh.

"Please don't hurt Emily," I repeated soberly, needing to secure her
safety above all else. "Please don't let anyone hurt her."

It felt like a tall order. Begging this Mafia man to provide protection for his hostage's baby. Who was I to even ask? He couldn't
possibly care. Rubbing my wrists was sweet and unexpected, but
going out of his way to make sure Emily was okay was something else.

I remained on edge, wondering again if that call was legitimate. If
Emily's location was something someone from the Rossini outfit had
to know.

"Does that call make you think she's in danger?" he asked as he
zipped up.

It was like he'd read my mind. "No? Maybe. I don't know. But
please, if you can spare my life, spare hers too. I need my daughter to

grow up knowing love and the little goodness that still exists in the world. That's all I want."

He snorted. "I thought you agreed that *I'm* the one in charge here, that we're going to do what I want."

I swallowed, wondering how else I could beg. I had nothing to barter. Nothing to offer. The desperate sensation of being hopeless and powerless gutted me.

He'd distracted me from worrying about Emily. Shoving his dick into me as another attempt to shake out more intel had definitely pulled my attention away from stressing about Emily. Now that the sex was done and the afterglow had faded, my baby was at the fore-front of my mind with clarity.

I watched as he paced back and forth through the room. Massaging my wrists felt good, but I couldn't relax. He'd untied me, but I knew I wouldn't get far if I tried to bolt for the door.

Ivan didn't lose that terse and pensive expression as he strode to and fro. Over and over, he stalked and seemed to be deep in thought. Or surrounded with decisions to make about this situation.

He glanced at me in passing, considering me with a critical eye. "You are staying here, Becca. I can't let you go."

"But Emily—"

"No. I told you. Every hostage has a purpose. Yours is to lure your father out of hiding."

I couldn't help the laugh that bubbled from my lips. It burst out, almost hysterical. "Steven doesn't care about me."

He grunted, shaking his head. "It doesn't look like it."

I stiffened. "What does that mean?"

"*I* ask the questions around here."

Lowering my face, I sighed and wished he could see that I wasn't trying to fight. I'd submitted. I acquiesced. I got the point. He was dominating this situation, and I wasn't about to usurp that.

"He hasn't reacted to the calls about your being held captive."

I lifted my hand as though to say *see!*

"But maybe he could be interested in your daughter."

I shook my head. "Emily? No. I doubt it."

"Not to be a doting grandpa. As leverage. Since the kid is Dominic Rossini's."

I shrugged. "I guess so."

He gave me a hard look. "No guessing about it. Your kid would be an important leverage if Murphy wanted to mess with the Rossinis. The baby would be another member of the Rossini bloodline."

I twined my fingers together, wringing them anxiously. "Please, I beg you. No, I demand. You have to keep her safe. If I'm stuck here to lure Steven out, then can you bring her to me?"

I couldn't understand how or why Emily would matter in this mess. Dom never acknowledged her. That dimple-cheeked infant was *mine* and no one else's.

"You can't go. I need you to stay here and be a part of my plan. Your father needs to be stopped."

"But can't you bring her to me?" I stood, getting into his face. "Please! I'm not asking to leave for the sake of freedom. I'm not asking you to look the other way. I just need to know Emily is all right. To see her and hold her and *know* no one has used her as any kind of leverage."

He grabbed his shirt and unwound it. "This isn't a fucking daycare."

I stepped closer, not caring about my nudity. Rage cloaked me in a fine garment, and I soaked it up as I fought back, shoving at his chest. "I didn't ask to be here! I never got involved. I wasn't standing around hoping I'd be taken against my will."

He deflected my pushes, holding my hand off to the side as I fumed. "I never asked to be a part of your damn plan."

My phone rang in the other room, pausing me from railing against him and his easy deflections of my hits. We froze, staring at each other as the ringtone reached us.

"Answer it," he ordered, tugging me by the hand into the hall where I could see the device lighting up on the table.

He stood next to me as I answered, fear strangling me as I read the name.

63

Hannah. I knew she'd be worried, and I had no clue what I would even say.

"Hello?"

"Becca!" She cried, groggy but alarmed. "I—I think someone knocked me out. I opened the door and..." She gasped. "Someone hit me on the back of my head. I just woke up. I'm still on the floor next to the pack-n-play."

"Is Emily okay?" I asked, begging her to confirm that my sweet baby was firm.

"Becca... She's gone!"

9

IVAN

"Gone?" Becca clutched the phone until her knuckles turned white. "Hannah! What do you mean she's *gone?*"

She slumped forward, her tone hysterical with this news that her baby was missing.

I reached out, instinctively reacting to guide her to fall on the couch, not the floor. Being near weakened women wasn't anything new for me, but this deep and automatic need to see to Becca's comfort and safety was something new.

We'd reached an impasse, her and I. In the middle of fucking her for the purpose of getting some damn answers—ones I suspected she might not actually have for me—I'd fallen into something other than doing my duty and job. With her pussy snug on my dick, her breathy moans all for my ears and her sweet surrender my reward, something bigger developed between us.

I wasn't lowering my guard so far that I was falling for her. There was no chance of her getting to me and convincing me to give her up, let her walk free. But while she was stuck here to serve as a bait, it seemed that the lines were blurring.

I *cared*. I was starting to. Hearing and seeing her so distressed about her child taunted me to empathize, to try to understand and make sense of it.

I'd never considered having a family outside of my brothers. For so long, I'd been convinced there was no woman out there who'd tolerate my darkness.

But she did.

What we did was just touching the surface of what I preferred, the basics of my kinks, but Becca not only accepted it, she'd reveled in it.

I had no experience with children to truly grasp how her world was crumbling apart with the news of Emily being gone. But I could suspect how terrible it was. If my sisters-in-law had their children already, if Mila and Amy had given birth to my nieces and nephew due soon, I would move heaven and hell to secure those children's safety.

Scuffling noises sounded on the other line, then a hard grunt and Hannah's scream.

Becca whimpered, staring at the cell phone as though it were a bomb ticking. Anxious and holding her breath, she clutched it and waited.

"Ivan. Get over here."

I took the phone at Dmitri's order. How and why *he* was answering, I didn't know.

"What's going on?"

"Get to her apartment. Yusef was tracking someone nearby, and another soldier was still watching her place."

He was running, his footsteps loud from the other line.

I headed to the door, too, aware of Becca hurrying after me.

"No. You stay here."

"But—" She grabbed my sleeve, eyes wide with panic as she struggled to keep up.

"The soldier watching her place alerted me to the invader. Fuck!" More scuffles sounded. "Just get here. Now!"

The call was dropped, and I thrust the phone at Becca. She fumbled to catch it, mouth open wide and spluttering for me to wait for her as I ran toward the door.

"Ivan! Wait! I need to—" A wretched sob cut her off as I warded her back.

"You have to stay here."

It could be a trick, a ploy to get her to run from here. Anything was possible. I had too few clues and answers, but I knew nothing would change the fact that she had to remain here as my hostage.

Maybe it's Murphy. Maybe he's stupid enough to try to turn the tables and get Becca to escape for her baby.

I slammed the door shut after me, ignoring Becca's cries and furious shouts to let her go. To bring her with me as I rushed out to meet with Dmitri and take charge.

One stern glance at the soldiers outside the door was all I needed to know she wouldn't be going anywhere. Despite her yells and fists banging on the door. No matter how much she begged and ordered, Becca would not be the first hostage to slip away from me. Those two men would stand there at the door and prevent her from leaving or anyone entering.

Familiar with Becca's address from staking out her home, I made quick work of driving over and seeking out my brother. I found him easily. In the alley, he and another Valkov soldier chased down another man, and I didn't hesitate to sweep in and join them in their efforts.

"Ivan. Watch out!" Dmitri's warning didn't make sense until the Italian swung around. He still held something, a black, bulky container I didn't recognize.

The instant wail of a cry startled me, though.

A baby.

Emily.

She was strapped into the container, a bucket-like carrier. In the blurred frenzy of too much action, I couldn't slow down time to get a good look at her. All that mattered was this man trying to steal her away.

I yanked the handle of the carrier, pulling the baby out of his grasp as I punched the asshole hard.

He staggered back, dropping out of my reach, but I wasn't done.

One-handed, as I held the carrier out of harm's way, I leaned up to kick the side of his head.

The carrier left my grip. I spared a single glance back to see that the Valkov soldier was taking it and setting it aside while I rained down more punches and kicks on this fucker.

Dmitri took over, holding up his hand to keep the Italian down. "Is that hers?" He panted from the exertion of chasing this man down from the building, and I retreated to see the infant screaming and crying. All that noise would cause more attention, and I hurried with the buckles and straps to get her out and shut her up.

I had zero instincts with an infant. I didn't know what the fuck I was doing, but I hoped to quiet her right now.

Before I could get her out and hold her, assuming that would help, I felt a rubbery piece of a circle. *What's this?* A pacifier? Something like it. I slipped it toward the baby's mouth, and she closed her trembling lips around it. Her green eyes were wide open and glossy as she stared at me with a pout. Fuck me. It was a punch to the gut, seeing Emily's innocent face so scared, her tear-streaked cheeks.

Dammit.

Guilt swamped me, and it made no sense. I'd never spent *any* time around kids. Never wanted to. Hadn't ever planned to. But after one second of seeing this sweet girl so upset, I wanted to pulverize this asshole who'd tried to take her.

Another soldier ran up, slowing in the alley.

"What the fuck is going on?" I demanded. He was the one who should've been watching around here.

"The Rossini broke into her place." He swallowed, catching his breath. "Marcus ran inside to intervene, and the footage shows the man breaking into Murphy's apartment."

I tensed, watching the baby. Hearing someone reference Becca by her surname bothered me. That was how I referred to her father, Steven Murphy, and I didn't like the association of Becca with him.

"He knocked out the babysitter. Marcus is with her, taking her to the hospital and telling her not to speak about this with anyone. Her head hurts, but it doesn't look bad. She's more startled and confused than anything. She was about to take the baby with her to drop off something at the college campus, taking the baby with her because she didn't know where the mother was."

I nodded, calming as the report clicked and made sense. Hell, I hadn't known about Emily. If I had, I would've planned to retrieve Becca and her daughter as a package deal. Two hostages for one. I hated the thought that she'd been suffering this whole night and worried about being parted from her daughter. Hannah was there, and it sounded like the sitter wouldn't have left the baby alone when Becca didn't come home. Still, it was a wrench in the plans I hadn't accounted for.

"Rossini?" I checked, standing as I lifted the baby carrier. I handed Emily over to the soldier as I studied the man. He looked Italian, all right, and livid. Caught between two Valkov men as they held his arms back, the asshole panted and scowled at me.

"Rossini?" I said again, asking him directly.

"Fuck you." He spat at my feet, and Dmitri slammed his fist into his stomach.

"Take him to the basement of the Garrent facility," I ordered, referring to a nearby Valkov property. The old warehouse would do for an impulsive torturing session.

I brought Emily to my car, and as the soldier slid into the backseat and tried to strap her in, I caught the baby's careful, scared gaze. She watched the man, sucking on that pacifier, and I felt hit once more with this possessive streak of rage. To fight for her. To defend her. To shelter her.

What the hell is happening? I rubbed at my chest, thrown off with how immediately I wanted to protect this stranger's baby.

No, not a stranger. Becca was no longer just a hostage. She was infiltrating my mind and tricking me to think of her as something far more personal.

"What are we going to do with the baby?" the soldier asked as Dmitri and the other man drove the Rossini to the building.

"*I* will handle her," I told him.

I did. I carried the handle to the seat-like contraption, confused with the awkward grip. Like a large loop, it jutted up and out. This wasn't ergonomic at all, but I kept her close, surrounded by Valkov men, as Dmitri brought the Rossini to the basement.

Dismissing the stains of blood dried on the floor, I set the carrier off to the side in a room with windows that permitted a view into the torture room. Emily whimpered but didn't cry out as I stepped away and closed the door to prevent any screams or sounds from bothering her too much. A Valkov man stood on guard in there with her, an older soldier. "Go on. I'll calm her if she fusses." He had a few kids of his own, so I knew he'd try his best.

I nodded, grateful for the assistance.

Then I strode out to the other room, extracting my knife from my pocket. Holding it reminded me of how I'd used it on Becca, but I shoved down the memory. Now wasn't the time. I had to focus. "Start talking," I ordered the Rossini.

He didn't. Not at all. I was careful with the wording of my questions. How I posed them could potentially give away information, so I began with general demands for him to explain what he was doing and why.

He said nothing, though, and after a while of punching him, severing his fingers and scalping him, I wondered if he even was a Rossini. He didn't bear the branded mark many of their soldiers wore as a sign of initiation into their organization, but whoever he was, whatever organization he affiliated with, he would not speak up.

Similar to Becca's silent treatment, the man who tried to take Emily remained mute. Silent to the point of pain and bleeding out. Quiet with a stubborn stupidity that pissed me off.

"He's not going to say shit," Dmitri concluded after a couple of hours.

I shook my head, agreeing with my brother but irked. All this time, and he wouldn't crack. It happened sometimes, but it aggravated me at the moment more than it otherwise should have.

Emily had fallen asleep, sucking on that pacifier, and I sighed as I glanced through the window at her on the table in that other room. She hadn't stirred.

Dmitri lifted his gun to point at the man, but I held my hand up to stop him.

I didn't need a gunshot to wake Emily. Instead, I returned to the man and sliced his neck.

While Dmitri gave orders to have the place cleaned up, another man approached to report in. "I've handled the other woman. She's at the hospital, and with concerns of a head injury, amnesia can help explain away what she saw." He handed over a large bag. "She won't talk, too scared, but we'll keep a man on her to make sure she doesn't report Becca and Emily missing."

I nodded, not taking the bag while using a handkerchief to wipe the blood from my hands. "What's that?"

"The woman was preparing to bring the baby with her to turn in an assignment due for a class. She had a bag of diapers and baby stuff prepared."

Probably thinking she'd need to stick with Emily all night.

"We have a crew cleaning up the break-in at the apartment building. Someone is altering the security footage as well."

"Good." I took the bag, sighing as I looked back at Emily. This was how things went down. We came, we saw, and we conquered. As a family, we worked together to deal with whatever shit came at us. I had complete faith in my men, in these soldiers who'd erase evidence of Becca and Emily being missing.

Now, I had to bring Emily to my hostage. There was no question in my mind to unite the mother and daughter. Keeping them separate served no purpose. Becca was a hostage to lure Murphy out, but she didn't need to suffer any undue stress of missing Emily and worrying about her.

On the drive back to my building, I peeked again and again at Emily sleeping in the backseat. This need to see her and check on her felt weird, but I couldn't stop.

Becca's pleas for me to make sure her baby was safe kept replaying in my mind, and I looked forward to being able to deliver on that request. I led a violent life, but I wasn't so cruel as to hurt an innocent baby. My wrath and anger were best suited for adults, for the men and women who threatened my family.

Calming down from the rush of torturing and killing that man, I considered too many questions that I couldn't answer. Intrigue filled me, and I tried to filter through all the new things to figure out.

How the hell is an innocent infant mixed up in the middle of all this?

Is she? Maybe she isn't.

It could all be a decoy.

Murphy could be trying to use her as a decoy. A diversion.

To what? Get Becca away from me so I couldn't get to him? He had to be aware of how I was hunting him down now, if I hadn't made it clear enough. Murphy was a long-standing enemy of the Valkov Bratva, but the men I supervised had let word slip that I was after him now.

What could I be missing? One more look back at Emily filled me with more confusion. This baby was a surprise, but I didn't want to linger in wondering how and if she mattered in this vendetta against Murphy. Of if she played a part in whatever Murphy was trying to do with the Rossinis.

After I parked and carried Emily up to Becca in my penthouse, I couldn't shake this paranoia that I was being watched. Not in this building, but in the city. Trying to hide Becca and Emily here seemed like a challenge, and I wished I could have more distance from any potential danger here.

Someone trying to reach Emily was a conflict I didn't want to worry about. Keeping the mother and daughter together would make it harder for anyone to sneak in and interfere. Distancing them from this epicenter of the city would be a smart move to keep things in my control, further from any Rossini or Murphy himself. While I intended to keep Becca as a hostage to lure Murphy out of hiding, I didn't plan to have him approach me *here*, at home or wherever Becca was. I'd arrange for a neutral meeting point, somewhere else for him to speak with me for his killing blow.

My building was guarded. This was a safe location. No one was getting in or out without my knowing about it. But it no longer seemed like enough.

Keeping Becca as a hostage was critical. But seeing to her security seemed like a more important responsibility that I didn't want to mess up. She had to be safe and secluded not only to lure Murphy out, but also because I needed to know she was all right.

"Ivan?" Her quiet greeting came as soon as I set foot in the penthouse.

Walking toward me, she watched as I turned and revealed the baby carrier. She had to have been waiting and watching the door all this time because as she ran toward me, crying tears of relief at seeing Emily, she looked one step away from collapsing from exhaustion.

Too bad. Now wasn't the time to relax or rest.

"Get ready. We're leaving."

She hurried to unbuckle Emily, glancing up at me.

"I don't trust staying here or being in the city," I explained. I didn't answer to her. I didn't need to tell her a damn thing, but I wanted to soothe her. I wanted to erase that etched-in expression of tension.

Seeing her in the throes of passion and pleasure would have been nice too, but I caught myself from thinking about fucking her again.

I wondered if I'd erred to do so in the first place. Because it was becoming too easy to see her as my woman, not my hostage.

BECCA

"Leaving?"

My fingers shook as I hurried to get Emily out of the carrier, amazed and overwhelmed with relief that she was here. My shoulders drooped as I pulled her up, waking her. She stirred, pouting and sucking quicker on her pacifier as I unbuckled her. Her tiny fists reached toward me, her fingers uncurling to grab me. Her eyes opened, blinking away sleep as I lifted her into my arms.

Ivan caught me off guard, telling me that I was going anywhere. After his repeated instructions that I was to stay here as his hostage, this news seemed like a contradiction I couldn't keep up with.

He was in charge. There was no doubt about that. Yet, it seemed so different for him to announce that something was happening, that I could anticipate being relocated.

I didn't care. It didn't matter to me where he took me so long as I would stay with Emily. Being reunited with my baby calmed me like nothing else could. Snuggling her tiny body, holding her up to my chest and breathing in her sweet baby smell, I relished the familiar weight of her. She filled that aching hole in my chest, proving that she was alive and well. Every minute that I had been held here against my will, I'd worried so deeply and without pause.

In the back of my mind, I knew she would be all right. Hannah was an excellent sitter. She had a big heart and never failed to go above and beyond my expectations. When I didn't come home when she thought I would, she had to have been worried and scared, confused too. But I never wondered if she'd leave or abandon my baby. I knew that Emily was in good hands and would remain with Hannah until I returned or she received an explanation for my absence. Hannah would have stuck with Emily no matter what.

Until she was taken.

"What's going on? What happened to Emily? Is Hannah okay?" The memory of my sitter's scream returned to my mind as I blurted out all the questions.

Ivan didn't seem ready to answer any of them. He shook his head as he walked further into the penthouse apartment.

I blinked, staring after him as I hugged Emily. He expected me to just accept my daughter's arrival and not wonder what was going on?

"I don't trust staying in the city right now."

It was an answer I hadn't expected, but I considered what he gave me. He moved quickly through the apartment, and I watched him closely. He gave me freer rein, no longer locking me in that room, and I wondered where I would go next.

Does that mean it's not safe to even talk here anymore? What is he so suspicious about? If this place could be bugged, I didn't want to speak up and interfere.

I felt blessed, so relieved to have Emily back in my arms. Just seeing her and knowing she was all right soothed my weary soul. If he wanted to move us, fine. If he deemed it unsafe here, who was I to question him? I was in the dark.

He said I was a hostage, but not Emily. I doubted he could've counted on retrieving a baby for his plans against Steven, but I refused to question his motives about reuniting me with my daughter either.

He didn't pack a bag, and all I had were the clothes on my back and the phone that was still connected to the device that Dmitri used to track my calls and snoop through my phone.

Emily's diaper bag was packed, and as we hurried out of the apartment, flanked by men, I was curious how Ivan had come to obtain the bag of necessities. My curiosity nagged me, but I decided to hold off on my questions until we were in his car.

The entire way to his dark car was tense, but I made no moves to run. I didn't try to escape. A fleeting thought hit me that maybe I was safest with him. That when I begged him to keep my child safe without any grounds to expect anything of him, that he would be the ideal man to secure Emily's safety. Even though he'd fucked me really hard, he hadn't tried to hurt me for the sake of inflicting pain. Everything he did, he did to push me and ensure that I'd receive a deep sense of pleasure I had never truly experienced before.

I climbed into the backseat with Emily, aware of the other men following us. Ivan had a team, had competent backup. Knowing this operation, whatever it was, would work like a machine, I felt safer.

"What is going on?" I asked again, not counting on getting an answer.

He sighed as he drove, lifting his dark gaze to the mirror to look at me, then Emily before returning his focus to the road. "A man who might have identified himself as a Rossini broke into your apartment."

The news bothered me, and I set my hand on Emily's chest, feeling her heartbeat and inhalations as she slept again. "Is Hannah okay?" Other than a little blood splatter on the straps of Emily's carrier, she seemed completely normal.

"She was knocked out as she prepared to take Emily with her to turn in an assignment due at school. As soon as he took Emily, the man I placed to watch your home alerted my brother." He glanced up. "Dmitri."

"Why'd she scream? Is she all right?" Worry crept back in.

"Dmitri startled her. We've seen to her medical care, and another man will stay near Hannah to ensure she doesn't talk to anyone about what happened. She'll be secured."

I breathed easier, calmer in knowing my sitter would be all right.

He snagged me with a stern look. "Are you still confident Dominic is unaware that you gave birth to his daughter?"

I nodded, furrowing my brow. "Yes. He sent me away from Italy, and in the year that has passed, I've heard not a word from him. No call. Nothing. I never once reached out to him. Only this week did Steven call and lie about Dominic wanting custody of Emily." Scowling, I stared right back at him, channeling my anger to him by accident. "Dominic wouldn't give a fuck. And I can't see how or why he'd care to do anything about Emily now."

He nodded once, paying attention to driving again.

Many questions lingered on my mind, but he seemed to have closed down on me. Thinking. Wondering. Strategizing. I was in the dark. I was clueless about anything to do with Steven and the Rossinis, and I felt it best to shut up until he asked me something else.

I figured he would, but he didn't. Not on the hours-long drive out of the city. Not as he led me into a guarded and lavish vacation villa upstate.

For days, he left me to get acquainted with Emily in this strange place. Burning questions stayed bottled within me, but I didn't bother asking him. He was busy on the phone or gone speaking with more of those men. Besides, I was too busy trying to understand it all myself.

Taking care of Emily felt like a vacation. Out of my crummy apartment, treated with unlimited food and clothing that Ivan must have arranged to be delivered here, I almost felt... pampered, if isolated and locked up.

I didn't have to count servings and ration my money on meals. I wasn't obligated to report to work and suffer that endless guilt over not spending time with Emily.

It was bizarre and unsettling to assume this peaceful limbo could last.

I'm a hostage. Nothing more.

But for a moment, I'd felt like someone else entirely. When he'd taken me by surprise and fucked me so hard, distracting me from the trauma of being kidnapped and teased, I felt like a new woman. Desired and coveted. Treasured and treated to bliss.

He hadn't come close to touch me, let alone speak about that rabid lust we'd burned out that one time. And I felt like an idiot to cling to those thoughts.

Because I'm not his woman. I'm nothing but his hostage.

And I still couldn't understand why. If he thought Steven would care about me and want to come out of hiding to retrieve me, he was mistaken. My sperm donor would surrender me to get his way and ensure his profit.

Dominic wouldn't care about me either, if Ivan was holding me hostage to impact that Rossini leader. I clung to the assumption that Dom didn't know that I'd had his baby. No matter which way I looked at this confusing mess, I didn't see how Emily would be in the middle of this Mafia war. It made no sense.

Ivan didn't tell me anything, as wary of me as I was of him. It was almost as though he couldn't tell how to view me anymore. After that one time he'd fucked me at the apartment in the city—over two weeks ago—I couldn't understand what his intentions were, if they'd changed since he captured me. He hadn't raped me, but I made no mistake of acknowledging that he was in charge.

And I hated it.

As I tidied up from dinner, washing the dishes one night in my stay here, I tensed as he walked through the kitchen. I was always aware of him, noting how every room seemed smaller with his larger-than-life presence.

Emily fussed, and I worried that he'd be annoyed. Not once did he act in any way that suggested he hated having her around, but I couldn't ignore this guess that he wasn't exactly a kid-friendly sort of man. He was a criminal, a man used to lurking in sex clubs, someone without a dad bod or ease with being near a baby.

I struggled to finish the dishes and give her attention where she whined in her highchair that Ivan or someone on his staff had procured without a second thought.

"Hold on, baby girl. Just hold on a minute and let me—" A glass slipped in the sudsy water, and I gasped as shards sliced through the water in the sink. And my hand. I hissed in a breath and clutched the tender area between my thumb and finger.

"What happened?" Ivan asked, immediately there and looming over my shoulder.

"Uh." I swallowed, unused to his speaking to me after such a long spell of avoidance. "I dropped a glass and—"

Emily cried louder, unhappy about the lack of attention.

"Hold on, Emmy." I grimaced, glancing at her past him. "Hold on. I'm coming."

Ivan frowned, snatching a towel and pulling my hand out of the water. "Compress it."

I accepted the towel and held it down tightly, bewildered and partly awestruck as he hurried to Emily and picked her up.

"Quiet," he told her. "Be quiet." He didn't order it like he did to his men. He wasn't instructing her like an impatient, bossy adult and expecting her to listen. But it was all he could likely think of to say as a comforting response to her needing to be picked up.

He stepped aside from the table, cradling her in his arms. The sight of my baby against his bare chest did something to me. Something raw and primitive. Among that canvas stretched taut over his ripped muscles, his skin marked with tattoos and scars, she pressed her cheek to him and sniffled. Calming instantly, she peered up at him. Confused but maybe curious, Emily gazed up at Ivan as he tried to rock and sway in his step a little bit. His big hands held her securely, and as he looked down at her, continuing to tell her to stay calm and be quiet in that softened yet gruff voice of his, my heart absolutely melted.

Oh, God. My ovaries could explode at the sexy yet tender sight. Since I learned that I was pregnant, I knew she wouldn't ever have a fatherly figure in her life. Not a dad. Not a grandpa. Nor an uncle. No one but me. So seeing this mean grump handle her so delicately threw me off.

And had me wondering how he could soothe her so easily.

Or if he'd ever want to repeat a dose of his affection on *me*.

11

IVAN

I paced through the living room, peeking at Becca napping on the couch each time I passed her.

Or, rather, each time *we* passed her.

Emily patted, then grabbed at my hair. Her fingers were small but mighty as she gripped tight, testing how hard she could play.

Gritting my teeth, I reined in my annoyance and tried to turn my head to the side and discourage her. It hurt like a bitch, but if it made the baby happy, if it kept her quiet, whatever.

She blinked up at me, sucking on her pacifier as I held her. Gazing into her innocent eyes never failed to hit me hard.

What did kids—infants—think about?

What did she think of me?

Why did she want to be carried nonstop?

What was so bad about sitting down?

Did she see in color?

I Googled about a baby's vision last night, curious, and I got hooked on the fact that at birth, as eyes developed, they made out black and white, high-contrast pictures best.

Was that why she kept staring at my tattoos?

Questions and curiosities ballooned every time I stopped to think about what her perspective on her short life was so far. Being near a baby was a new experience, but it wasn't a bad one. Different, but not awful. Every time I tried to help Becca handle her with this fussiness, I learned how to hold her better, how to balance her in my arms and multitask. How to adjust to the slow way she seemed to want to take over my life.

Margie finally answered, and Emily reached for the phone again, giving up on my hair.

I shifted her to higher in my arms, keeping my phone between my shoulder and head.

"Hey, Margie."

"I am on vacation, sir..." she answered in a teasingly scolding tone.

"I know. But I need your help."

This housekeeper was the only motherly figure we'd had at the mansion for years. All of us brothers appreciated her help and guidance, and she was the first one I'd thought to call for help.

"With what, Ivan?" she asked.

"A baby. My... The..." I sighed. She could be trusted, but I simply didn't know what to call Becca anymore. While she remained locked here as a hostage, I had to face the possibility that she had been an ineffective one so far.

"A baby. She's teething, according to her mother, and..."

"Is her mother there?"

"Yes." I glanced again at Becca's sleeping form on the couch. "But she's tired and overwhelmed. She's been suffering from allergies, but maybe it's a cold. I just need some help with the baby."

"Hmm."

I could picture her now. Trying to see me dealing with a baby had to be a comical image for her. And yes, she was on vacation this week, but she hadn't actually gone anywhere. Mila insisted on her not working for at least five whole days because she feared the workaholic was burning out.

"Okay." Her reply came quickly.

"I'll arrange for transportation." I smiled as Emily grinned at me.

I'd kill a man who dared to witness this baby softening me up, but dammit, her charm was infectious.

"I have no doubt you already have someone coming to get me now," she quipped.

"Maybe."

We disconnected the call, but I bided my time walking with Emily. She wasn't heavy. I didn't have anything else to do until this evening, taking a call with Yusef to check in on any possible sightings of Murphy in the city.

As long as Becca napped and rested, I could do my best to preoccupy Emily, and it seemed that walking around was all she wanted. To be held. To see the house and gaze out the windows. But always in my arms.

"No wonder she's so tired," I muttered to myself, looking again to make sure Becca rested.

For the first three weeks, I did my best to avoid being near the redheaded woman who tricked me into wanting something that could never be. Out here at the vacation home, it almost seemed domestic. Like she was my woman, my mistress, my whatever I wanted to call her. Just *mine*.

I couldn't allow that kind of easement. I had to keep my guard up around her. I couldn't forget that she'd only come into my life as a hostage. If she were any other woman, I wouldn't have personally cared to stick around. Any other Bratva soldier would have done just as fine in my place. I could have arranged for anyone in the family to stand guard over her and Emily and make sure they stayed put under my control.

But I didn't. This need to be near her and see her was a stubborn urgency I couldn't tamp down. Even when I had the wisdom to step away and have a breather from her, I was drawn to return and know that she was here.

All those days blurred into an awkward tension until she'd cut her hand. Until that moment, I'd maintained a distance but failed to forget about her. That incident let me show her that I would try to help with Emily.

I hadn't missed her expression of surprise. I would never forget how stunned and interested she was to see me try to comfort Emily, as though she'd dismissed me as someone who could never appease a fussy baby.

I was no expert. But the kid did quiet down, often staring at me with blunt wonder to the point she stopped crying. Or she'd babble and hum, swat at my chest and shoulders.

Becca said she was teething and that she was impatient to walk, not crawl. In a quiet moment the day after she cut her hand, she admitted that she felt like she'd trained Emily to always want to be picked up. But she didn't care. She liked feeling needed and loved being able to cuddle her.

I understood what she meant. I felt like a king to calm Emily down, to pass her test.

While I almost felt like an idiot to lower my guard and go soft with the awareness of how hard it had to be for Becca to survive as a single mother, I couldn't help but want to reduce some of the burden off her shoulders.

She wasn't working. Her job was probably already replaced. But being a mother of a fussy baby *was* a job. A full-time one, plus the immaculate orderliness she maintained of the vacation house out here. Cooking, laundry, and even general cleaning up and dusting around the house.

Margie would take over. She'd fuss over Emily. She'd insist that Becca relax. And I looked forward to the woman finally having a break and letting her body get over her slight illness, whether it was just allergies or a cold.

Walking with Emily made me sad, though, because I couldn't help but wonder if my father or mother ever did this for me or my brothers. They'd doted on us. My father was a brave, generous man until Pavel killed him, but his duties were always priority over child-rearing. And my mother? She'd passed away so long ago, I hardly recalled her.

Who else do you have? I watched Emily as she rested against my chest, her eyes drooping as she grew sleepy.

My mother died too young and my father had been murdered too soon as well, but I never lacked for companionship. All four of my brothers were there for me, and they always would be. Under Alek's leadership as *Pakhan*, the Bratva returned to a family-oriented and cohesive unit.

Mila had married Alek. Amy was with Nik. Both women were bringing in the next generation of children.

And here, I could have a ready-made family within my reach. Becca and Emily. A wife and daughter. It didn't matter to me who donated sperm for Emily to be born. It mattered who showed up in her life. Who held her as she fussed. Who fought for her safety.

Who am I kidding?

Settling down wasn't a feasible option. Not for me. Being here out of the city was an illusion. This mansion wasn't a home, but a vacation spot that the Bratva owned. I wasn't here to play happy family and pretend that I could be an active parent to this baby. Becca wasn't a guest here for any reason other than baiting Murphy.

Settling down? With Becca?

I shook my head and rolled my eyes as I continued to walk and lull Emily to sleep.

She would never want *me*. Not really. Even though she'd shown me how readily and eagerly she could follow my lead sexually and come apart so beautifully in my arms, under my hand, and around my dick, I knew what happened there.

In the heat of the moment, she'd caved. At that precise opportunity, when she was vulnerable, shocked, and traumatized by all that had happened, she'd given in to me.

I'd manipulated her. I'd forced her so far, but in the end, she'd wanted it. She fought me, but not when I slammed my dick inside her. She'd been tied up, but she hadn't struggled to escape my touch. The slickness of her pussy was evidence of how turned on she'd been when I took her roughly.

But for anything else? She'd be smarter to resist me. I was too hard of a man for someone as "normal" and nice as her.

I liked it hard, all the time. I preferred toys and bondage. Voyeurism and pain.

She'd struggled to last a handful of minutes at that club, and I wasn't under any illusion that she could compromise to be more like me, to fit in with my depraved preferences and kinks.

Wanting her again but knowing how dumb it would be to act on it, I'd kept my distance. These three weeks had been a personal torture of knowing Becca was close but not for me.

And at this point, it gnawed at me when this tension and slowly building desire would snap.

So far, nothing was happening. Dmitri and Yusef helped most with tracking Murphy in the city, and he wasn't biting at any of the news that Becca had been taken. Nothing came in from our spies with the Rossinis, either.

While the wait for a development could take time, I felt like I was running out of it where my restraint lay with Becca.

My phone rang, and I shifted the now-napping Emily in my arms to answer. The screen told me it was Maxim, and I wondered what he'd have to tell me.

"I think we might need you to drive to the city," he said after we greeted each other.

"Now what?" I perked up, though I kept my voice low. "Something come in about Murphy?"

"No. The cops are heading to one of the clubs." The emphasis he put on those words, *the clubs*, signaled which establishments he was speaking about. The sex clubs. The ones I supervised.

"Which one?"

"LeVant's."

Huh. That was a pricy place, secure and hard to get into. LeVant's was easily the Bratva's most secretive sex club, and few knew how to get through the doors. It was a selective, carefully monitored clientele there, and I doubted I wanted the cops poking around for long. The more secretive the club and the clientele there, the higher the profits.

"What's going on there?" I asked, praying Margie would get here soon so I could leave to deal with business. It would have been nice for something to happen with this hostage situation and luring Murphy to reveal himself, but it wasn't as though I could forgo or slack in my usual duties.

"It sounds like people are getting drugged."

I furrowed my brow. *That's it?* Drugs were commonplace in the Bratva, and at the clubs, too.

"And it sounds like it's a complicated situation," Maxim reported. "Alek wanted to check it out himself, but he and Nik are dealing with something else downtown. Dmitri's chasing a lead, and since LeVant's falls under your lead..."

"Yeah. Okay. I got it." I didn't need a lecture. "I appreciate having a heads up."

I doubted it would be anything bad, but still, I had to check it out.

As carefully and quietly as I could, I lowered Emily to Becca. Her arms slid over the baby, almost as though her body recognized the press of hers even in sleep.

Mother and daughter slept on, peaceful and quiet, and I stalled for a moment. I committed the angelic image of them like this, safe and sound, to memory and wished that it was a picture I could come home to every day. Every night.

As the front door opened and Margie entered, calling out for me quietly, I sighed and scowled.

Becca was a hostage.

Every hostage had a purpose.

And Becca's would not be to fill a gap I hadn't ever realized before.

As my woman.

12

BECCA

I lowered my head toward the freshly ladled bowl of soup, inhaling the warmth and delicate fragrances until my skin felt damp from the steam tickling my cheeks and lips.

Oh. So, so good. It wasn't a foolproof solution for this nagging sinus pressure, but it felt heavenly. And so different. New. No one had ever cooked a meal for me. Not since my mother died in a car accident when I was seven. I supposed the hospital food I received when I was there for all forty-seven hours of labor for Emily's birth could count as warm food someone else had prepared for me, though. My standards were low. I'd learned to lower the bar.

"How is that?" Margie asked.

I smiled up at her, open and trusting of her generosity.

Or more like Ivan's generosity. It was hard to remember that I was supposed to be a hostage here. I felt like a pampered princess. The man secured a long-term housekeeper to "help me out" with Emily. That was the single sweetest and most thoughtful thing a human had *ever* done for me.

Procuring me hired help.

Margie was a godsend. When I woke from my nap, I was a bit startled to hear the portly woman humming and dusting. She'd identified herself as the Valkovs' favorite housekeeper and soon-to-be godmother, and I wondered if she was a figment of my imagination.

"He asked me to help you out, you poor girl. How long have you been sniffling like that?" That was how she'd explained her presence, and I knew better than to protest.

With her company, bustling around, cleaning the kitchen and generally being helpful, she showed me what I'd been missing all my life.

Support. Companionship. Something a lot like motherly love that I'd gone without for almost my whole life.

"The soup?" I asked, holding my necklace pendant back so it didn't hang low as it slipped out from under my shirt and knocked against the bowl I hunched over. "It's *perfect*, Miss Romanov, just perfect."

She tsked. "Nonsense. I'm not a Romanov," she playfully scolded. "The second Ivan's grandfather saved me from the abusive man I'd been arranged to marry, I considered myself a Valkov."

The pride in her protest was strong.

"Just call me Margie. I insist."

I grinned, breathing in another deep inhale of the scented steam from the most decadent chicken noodle soup I've ever had. She'd whipped it up in seemingly no time at all, chatting with me in the kitchen all the while.

She didn't interrogate me. Her questions were casual and calm, for no other reason than making me feel comfortable with her sudden presence here at this huge, expensive house.

"I can't believe you've been trying to clean this all yourself," she commented. "Those boys don't vacation out here often. This place has been sitting here collecting dust for months and you're putting your all into it."

"Well, between naps..." I shrugged. "I've never liked being idle. There's money to be made. Things to clean and fix."

She laughed once, cooing at Emily as she gnawed on an iced piece of celery. The woman was right. My daughter wasn't great at tearing off chunks to choke on, just mushing it and keeping it attached with the strings to soothe her gums.

I'd only gotten a catnap earlier, but with this comfort and peace Margie instilled in me, with her magical touch of calming Emily and not letting me be frazzled with her fussiness, I felt tired again—in a good way. I could recognize the difference now. Instead of feeling exhausted and at my wit's end, I was content.

Since I learned I was expecting Emily, I'd worked. And worked. And worked some more. As a single mother handling sixty-hour workweeks, piecing in teeny slips of time for my art, and being a solo parent, I was overdue for a break.

Under Margie's urging, I lay back on the couch and watched Emily play and babble to herself within the collapsible playpen Ivan had purchased just for her.

She never had this much space to crawl and play at our apartment. She could practice pulling herself up and falling without worrying about landing on our hard floor but on plush carpet instead.

Seeing her happy and calm eased my mind, and I slipped into another nap, wondering if I had to wake up from what felt like a dream.

Before long, I was woken. Beeps pulled me from the nap, and I blinked my eyes as I felt for my phone. I'd kept it nearby, anxious in case Ivan would want to contact me when he left for "business" matters. He was a Mafia man. I didn't want to know what "business" meant to him. The less I knew, the better. Yet, I couldn't give up on this hope that he'd *want* to contact me. That he'd miss hearing my voice.

"Oh, stop dreaming already." He'd captured me and held me as a hostage, but he wasn't a heartless brute. He'd made me come. He brought my daughter to me. He provided baby things without question, replenishing clothes and necessities for me. Arranged for a housekeeper to assist me.

If a man ever wanted the quickest way to impress a single mother and find the easiest way into her heart, it was in the action of providing a capable woman like a grandmotherly fairy as backup.

No one could fault me for forgetting that I was a hostage here.

Still, the anxiety of wondering if and when Murphy would reveal himself ate away at me. Because if and when he did come out of hiding... I would have to leave. Ivan hadn't lied. He'd told me that I was sticking with him for only one reason.

Which doesn't explain why he'd fucked me...

I grabbed my phone, blinking at the screen. The number that read out snapped me awake, and I sat up, alert.

Dmitri had called this number "interesting" that first night. He'd led me to believe the call came from a Rossini address, but I had yet to be convinced that the caller was someone affiliated with Dom.

The beeps signaled a blank text. "Huh?"

I lacked the time to set the phone down. It rang again, the same number, but this time as an actual call.

"Hello?"

"Becca."

I grimaced at his voice. Every day, I woke up wishing I never had to deal with him ever again.

"What do you want, Steven?" He wasn't disguising his voice this time. Knowing he was calling from that same number as before, I now understood that he'd been the one identifying as a Rossini. Falsely.

"Where are you?" Of course, he didn't answer my question. He never did. Any communication with me was for his benefit, not mine.

"What?"

"Where. Are. You?" He sighed, like I was the problem here.

I narrowed my eyes. I hadn't spoken with him since that time he called when I was at the gallery, when he wanted me to get that envelope at some club.

"Where?" he shouted, and I cringed at the decibel of his order. A glance at Emily napping on the floor calmed me. His shout wasn't that loud beyond the reach of my phone's speaker hole, but it *felt* like a bellow.

"Why do you want to know where I am? What's it to you?"

"Stop playing games. Tell me where."

Narrowing my eyes, I stood and walked away from the spacious living room with the play pen. I stepped further from Emily, unable to shed this hunch that he wasn't calling to ask where I was or where

Emily was, but to learn the location of Ivan. I didn't need to be told in a lecture or dissertation about how the Valkovs were enemies of my father. I got it. I understood the rules from what Ivan had expressed in wanting to capture me as bait to make Steven come out of hiding.

Maybe this is the moment he will.

"Becca!" He grew impatient with my silence.

"I'm not telling you anything."

But maybe you will. As I considered how smart it would be to record this call, I hurried toward the kitchen.

Margie raised her brow as I hurried there, but she didn't scare easily. She waited patiently as I gestured at my phone as I set it to speaker, mouthing, *where is your phone?*

She handed her phone over without question. After she unlocked it, I quickly went to the video app to record.

"I'm not telling you anything, Steven," I repeated as the video rolled.

Doing this showed my loyalty. It felt strange to align with Ivan, but at the same time, it felt too right. Ivan was a stranger. I'd been in his company for three weeks now, but I knew with an instinctive strength that I would side with him.

Ivan was more caring for me than my father had ever been. Ivan wasn't conning me. He'd told me upfront that I was a hostage in this situation, that he needed me here because he was after my father.

Ivan was more considerate than Dom, too. This Mafia man was honest about his plans, and he was caring, deep down, when he pleasured me.

I wanted to help Ivan and his family, not Steven. No guilt struck me at the thought of throwing my parent under the bus like this. Steven would deserve anything and everything coming his way for his choices, for his mistakes. That was how karma worked. I wasn't in the wrong, and I felt nothing but wise to lean on Ivan for security despite his claiming I was a thing with a purpose.

"You don't have to tell me anything, you stupid whore. I know you're with Ivan. You've been taken by the Valkovs."

I licked my lips, eager to keep him on the line. "Why would you think that?"

He laughed darkly. "I don't *think* it. I know it. You never called for help. That was the first clue that tipped me off."

Margie pressed her lips together, watching me as I rubbed the clay pendant on my necklace. I felt it, grounded by the familiar smooth surface as I listened to Steven.

"I know because the Valkovs killed the man I tasked with taking your bastard baby."

I stiffened, and Margie narrowed her eyes, not seeming to like the sound of that.

He had arranged for Emily to be snatched away? I'd never, ever forgive him. He could die a slow death and rot in hell for *ever* daring to compromise my daughter in anything dangerous.

"I know because I saw you through the windows of his fucking apartment." He laughed once again. "Never forget that I have many friends with eyes and ears all through the city."

But not here? Outside of it? "And just as many enemies," I snarled.

"Tell me where, Becca."

I glanced at the device attached to my phone. Dmitri had done something to it, and I wondered if it disabled my location.

"Tell me where you are."

I owed him nothing. I felt indebted to Ivan, not him. I didn't care what Steven wanted. It had nothing to do with me. My only goal was to provide for my baby the best I could, and only my association with Ivan enabled me to feel like I was doing a decent job of it.

"Fuck off." I crossed my arms. Damned if he thought I would ever give him a chance to screw with me or my child again. Now, more than ever before, he was dead to me, a threat, an adversary to keep far away.

"What?" He chuckled without humor, teasing me. "What is it? You think you're falling in love with this guy now too?"

I bit my lip, tense with rage. He thought it was so hilarious, mocking how I'd thought I had a real relationship with Dom. I didn't have "anything" with Ivan, either. I was his pawn, his hostage, but unlike Dom, I wanted a very real commitment with Ivan.

"Are you trying to protect him?" Steven taunted. "You want to be a good girl for Ivan and hope he likes you more than Dom ever did?"

I clenched my teeth together so hard that it hurt my jaw.

"Just tell me where you are!"

Emily's cries cut through the quiet. She'd woken in the other room, and I bet she was scared, not seeing me and being in a still-unfamiliar place alone.

Margie frowned, going for her, but I held my hand up and stopped her.

"Fuck you, Steven." I would never tire of echoing my truest, most heartfelt sentiment with him.

He growled. "I'm warning you, you stupid cunt. Do not try to cross me."

He hung up, and I turned with Margie to hurry to Emily and comfort her.

And seek her little arms wrapped around me for a semblance of comfort I needed after hearing from the man who called himself my father.

What I wanted, though, was to see Ivan and know if he would appreciate my decision to try to help his cause.

I would do anything to escape Steven's role in my life. Even deliver him to the Mafia men hell-bent on killing him.

13

IVAN

LeVant's seemed calm when I arrived. Nothing stood out as a concern. No cops milled around. During the drive that I'd had to endure to get here in the heart of the city and make my way through the hallways to reach the secret location, everything had settled.

"Tell me," I instructed the supervisor in charge tonight. Kenneth was a good man, a former soldier in the army who'd turned to the Bratva for a sense of belonging. He was the best man to keep an eye on things at one of the Bratva's most profitable sex clubs. LeVant's was in good hands when he was on the floor.

He shook his head, shrugging. While he stepped aside to speak with me, he maintained a close eye on the clientele and staff here. The man never relaxed or lowered his guard, and that was why I felt confident that nothing bad had happened here while I was out playing house with Becca and Emily.

"A couple of guests were drugged." He mentioned their names, and that detail didn't alarm me. A pair of entitled, young socialite women. They were often wasted when they came here to party and look for a good time. I wasn't surprised.

"I was concerned with how quickly they went down." He furrowed his brow. "The Doms in the scenes with them seemed freaked out about how rapidly they'd fallen unconscious. Seizures too. But when they removed them and took them to the hospital, they seemed to improve."

"Did they run tox reports?"

He nodded. "I believe they are still waiting on results."

"What were they taking here?"

"Nothing, actually. Since those incidents last year with the older folks trying out the harder lines of coke, we've been careful."

I knew that. And he was correct. Drugs happened. The Valkov Bratva moved a lot of them, sometimes through clubs like this, but we were in the business to make money, not to kill anyone. We wanted customers coming back for more, not surviving to want another hit. Drugs would never disappear in this world, and if we could control some of the main transportation routes of them, we could see to them going where they should and not being abused by other organizations. We were far from saints, but money *did* make the world go round.

"It wasn't anything bad. Romeo was on the phone with Maxim when the women were found drugged in their rooms. But I was surprised when you showed up."

I patted his back. "I know you'd have it under control."

Still, Maxim seemed concerned. He wasn't often out in the field as much as Alek, Nik, Dmitri, and I were, so maybe he needed to hone his judgment about what was an emergency or not.

People got roofied, too. It happened no matter where people went to drink and party. It was a stark but true fact of life.

"Sorry to ruin your evening," Kenneth said respectfully.

I grunted. Ruin it? It wasn't his fault. All I'd been doing was staring at Becca when I thought she wasn't looking. And helping Emily not be so fussy. It seemed like I couldn't avoid bonding with that sweet baby, but I was relieved when Margie showed up to take over so I could leave.

Emily hadn't hesitated to reach for Margie to be held. Margie just had that quality of calm about her.

Driving into the city gave me a chance to try to get my head on straight where Becca was concerned. Distance helped, but I wondered if I was too far past the point of simply setting a buffer between us. I'd tried that for the first three weeks we'd stayed at the vacation villa upstate.

No matter how long it was between the times I saw Becca, I missed her. And regardless of whether I was in the city or just the next room in the house, I yearned to be near her again.

My body and heart were in sync with wanting her to a possessive depth of urgency, but my mind lagged behind. I knew I had no business trying to envision her as a permanent fixture in my life, but I couldn't stop thinking about her and wishing for another chance to enjoy her sweet surrender.

Seeing her as a mother of a baby changed my view of her. It didn't soften her, but it showed me that she was far more than just another pussy to fuck, just another woman to fill with my cum.

She mattered. She had the role of raising an innocent baby. And she did so with strength and determination that were damned sexy.

With every minute I spent at the club, walking around with Kenneth and dealing with other minor matters of supervision here, I registered the passage of time as another minute away from Becca. I worried all the while, stuck on the slightly paranoid thought that coming here—being away from her—was the goal.

Was it a diversion, trying to separate me from Becca?

Was this not-so-serious concern of drugs a way to distract me from something else?

But from what? For what?

Being away from Becca and Emily bothered me, and I wanted to assume my anxiousness to return to them was nothing to be concerned about. That I felt off and alert because I wasn't there to see them and know they were safe and under my watch and control.

And why isn't the fucker trying to get her back? The Bratva men had left plenty of pointed messages of Becca being held hostage by now. And still, the man hadn't bitten once.

Becca had scoffed that Steven Murphy, her father, didn't care about her, and I had to seriously consider whether that could be true.

But I wasn't ready to give up on keeping her as a hostage yet.

Whatever Murphy was plotting seemed to be a complicated and delicate scheme if he was determined to be this unreachable and stay hidden for so long. I had to wonder, again, who he was hiding from. What had he done to need to stay on the down low for his own safety? The fucker was as corrupted as they came. He could've gotten mixed up with any number of bad things and bad players.

Not knowing bothered me. If I knew what he was doing—with the Rossinis or anyone else—I'd be able to track him and finish him off once and for all. Or I could manipulate his foes to get him to react. The enemy of my enemy was my friend, but in this violent world, we were all fucking enemies at the end of the day.

"Trust me," Kenneth said in conclusion after we'd checked on all of the club. "This drugging incident tonight is *nothing* like what happened at Harrow's."

I nodded, thinking back to how the Cartel had attacked people at one of the Bratva's strip clubs. First, the Ortezes snuck in and shot a few guests. Then they escalated in an attempt to wound the Bratva by burning the whole place down.

The Valkov Bratva wouldn't fall because one of our many establishments had been scorched. Murphy had been tied to that incident, too. It was just one of a long list of infractions that cop had with us.

Being asked to come in and check on a report of two women being drugged was nothing like the loss of Harrow's and the reputation of the Bratva business being a target of the Cartel. What I faced here tonight—and what Kenneth had under control appropriately—was a hiccup compared to the strip club fire.

Still, I was on edge, wondering what I was missing.

Without any other way to describe it, this felt like the calm before the storm. A deceiving spell of peace that wouldn't last.

I didn't know if wanting and missing Becca had me off like this or if the delay and wait for Murphy to reveal himself was bugging me.

I couldn't shake this sensation of waiting for something bad to hit. And this report of drugged women wasn't that bad.

"Thank you for having everything under control," I told Kenneth before I left.

He nodded and smirked. "Of course. Of course. Are you heading out?"

"I am." *To get back to Becca.* I didn't have to stay with her at that house. The men guarding it would keep her and Emily safe there. Now that I'd made the drive into the city, it would make more sense to stay here. Maybe even hang out at the club and try to lose this grip Becca had on me without even trying to snare me or seduce me. According to what I'd told her, she was there as a hostage. It wasn't surprising that she wouldn't take the initiative to approach me.

But I suspected that I wasn't alone in this awareness. Any time I came into the room, she tensed. I felt her eyes on me, always watching. Any time I helped with Emily, she went quiet and watched me so carefully, so full of wonder and appreciation that I felt like I was impressing her. That I was fitting into her life as more than a criminal and thug who'd taken her.

She'd been so responsive to both my teasing with the knife and then when I'd lost control and fucked her hard. I still recalled with clarity how she'd cried aloud and sounded so sweetly blissed out.

"Veronica was asking for you specifically yesterday," Kenneth said, arching one brow.

I didn't reply, staring at him and knowing he wouldn't lie. Not about that. Veronica was a regular, loaded with money and an insatiable sex drive. If she wasn't at one of the Bratva's operated sex clubs, she'd be at another elsewhere. The older woman had no scruples about seeking out pain and pleasure, and to my knowledge, she'd never once uttered a safe word.

Long ago, I got a thrill out of sharing a room with her. Years ago. She'd entertained me with the notion that I could do whatever I wanted. I could fulfill my darkest, most depraved kinks. And she'd tolerated it—no, she'd thrived on it. At first, I realized she was an adrenaline and danger junkie, needing to be pushed too far to be turned on and let go. After a while, though, it lost its appeal.

Still, she claimed years ago that I was the "best" at making her happy.

I shook my head, rolling my eyes as I wondered about the woman ten years my senior. "What is she on, husband four or five now?"

He smirked. "Six, I believe."

We had dossiers and profiles for all the clientele at LeVant's. He wasn't gossiping. But that fact dissuaded me further from spending time with her.

Hell, I wasn't interested in spending time with anyone but Becca, and the lines were set too deep in stone to mark us as enemies, as untouchable.

"Have a good night," I told him as I left, not even bothering to comment on Veronica missing me at any club. I'd never given any guest, any subbie, any woman the impression that I was open for anything more than a singular, no-strings fling.

Except you. I thought of Becca with every mile that my car sped until I returned to the vacation villa.

I nodded at the guards patrolling as I entered, and I quietly locked the door behind me. All was silent, and I grinned to myself, pleased that asking Margie to come and help was the smartest thing I'd done in a long while. She was a godsend, ideal to help with any hardship or trouble. I wasn't shocked that she'd somehow helped fussy Emily stay down for the night.

Without making a noise, I headed for Becca's room. No matter how busy I was, no matter where I went or what I worked on, I *always* checked that she was sleeping. Some nights, I couldn't—when she was up trying to get Emily back to sleep and I was awake as well.

Tonight, she lay alone in her bed. Emily was in her room down the hall, near Margie's, I bet.

I stalled, watching Becca as she rested, and I felt comforted at seeing her content. Making her comfortable appeased something stupid in me, something that felt like too many messy emotions.

Something like love. And a man like me would never qualify in that department where she was concerned.

Instead of risking her waking and catching me spying on her, I turned and went to my suite. In the bathroom, I stripped and turned on the water, needing the soothing, pounding pressure of the water to clean me and also provide me with the lubrication to jerk off to the memory of her coming for me in the city.

I panted, breathing hard at the force of my orgasm, but I snapped out of the trance of bliss. A sound reached my ears, past the droning thrum of the water, aside from the fan spinning.

I tensed, turning my head to the side.

Right outside the door stood Becca, her red hair noticeable through the frosted surface of the door.

And she was staring right at me.

The idea of her catching me masturbating turned me on all over again.

Blinking once, twice, then wiping the water from my eyes, I wondered if it was a dream. Another fantasy.

It wasn't.

She stood there, and I smiled at what she might do if I yanked the door open and hauled her under the water in here with me.

14

BECCA

Ivan turned his head toward me. I couldn't make out everything through the opaque shower stall, but I registered that he pivoted to notice my presence.

Second thoughts crashed through. I had no business being here, seeking him out.

Several minutes ago, I heard a slight noise that somehow yanked me straight out of sleep, and I gave up lying in the darkness of my own room. After I got a glass of water from the kitchen, I caught the faint sound of water running from elsewhere in this huge, quiet house. Meandering down the hall, I saw the light on from the crack beneath Ivan's door.

Trespassing into his room seemed inappropriate. This urgency to tell him about Steven's call propelled me in there, though, seeking him out no matter how late it was.

Finding him in the shower and lingering just outside it was wrong.

Yet, nothing could tear me away. I was rooted right here, unable to tear my lusty gaze from the outline of his big body under the water in there.

I swallowed, feeling my cheeks burn as I realized he was aware of my looking at him.

Like a goddamn creeper, a deer caught in the headlights, I stayed still and immobile, unsure what to do.

Should I say something? I wanted to tell him about that call, but like this? After following my stubborn curiosity to sneak in here and see if he was home?

Desire ruled my actions. That and a weird sense of missing him and wanting him despite being a hostage here.

Should I run? Turn tail and hide in my room until we could go back to that funky avoidance that he'd started when we first arrived at this house?

I bit my lip as he moved forward, shutting the water off.

"Becca?"

I cleared my throat, burning up with more of a blush that he was naked. Right there. And not shouting at me to leave him alone like this.

"Um." I cleared my throat once more, trying to lose that croakiness of shame and feeling stuck. "Yeah."

"What the hell are you doing?" He didn't demand it like an order. I detected no trace of an accusation or insult in his tone, either. More than anything, he seemed confused and humored, curious.

What am I doing? Other than wishing I was in that shower stall and having you clean me with your tongue? Than imagining bending over so you can—

"Becca?"

I flinched, shaking my head. "I wanted to talk to you about something."

He reached for the door and shoved it open. "About what?"

"Earlier—" My voice died as he stepped out of the huge shower stall. Steam wisped out with his exit, curling around his magnificent yet battered body. I blinked, taking in the full frontal view of the most rugged body I'd ever seen. Scars and tattoos showed all over him, and something that looked like a branding mark near his pecs.

Oh, whoa.

I'd felt his body against mine that one time he fucked me hard and fast. But he was behind me then, depriving me of this view.

And I stared. I couldn't look away, taking in all the details of him wet and bare. Water streaked down over the bulges and ridges of his muscles, heightening how fit and strong he was. From the dripping strands of his dark hair, all the way down to his feet. Every inch of him was on display, and my pussy reacted at once.

I tensed, feeling the instant clench of desire deep in my abdomen. I felt slick, throbbing as my pulse kicked faster and the blood drained south to the tender flesh where I missed him most.

He cleared his throat, fully aware that I was staring and taking my time with it. Even though he grabbed a towel and rubbed it over his head, he made no move to cover up at all.

"Sorry." *Not sorry.* I lowered my gaze, staring at his toes instead. "I should…" I turned too quickly, stumbling against the towel rack anchored to the wall. "I, um…" I set my hand on the rod for hanging towels and tried to glance back at him.

My gaze fell right back on his huge dick, and I swore he thrust his hips out at me, enticing me to look my fill.

"I'm sorry." I covered my face with one hand, hating this blush that burned hotter. "I had no business coming in here. I just wanted to speak with you and I thought you were here and—"

"I am here." Whisking sounds of friction followed his motions of drying off.

"Right. Yeah. You're here." I swallowed, tormented with the lure of looking up at his huge cock, then up the lines of his abs, over his pecs, then his neck and his smirking face.

Desire swirled within me as the steam from his shower dissipated. I fought not to want him. I resisted this stubborn lust he inspired in me. Hiding it was futile, and I settled on praying he wouldn't notice. Or if he did, he wouldn't tease me about it.

I wanted him so badly, even though I knew I shouldn't be desiring someone like him. I was a hostage, a temporary fixture in his life until he found Steven and killed him. He wasn't a man I could count on forever, but at this moment, heated up and so full of longing for that deep bliss he'd pushed me to, I wondered if it would be so bad to tell him this truth. That I wanted him to the point of pain.

"So..." He tossed his towel to the side of the room, not at all modest. Passing me, he brushed against my side as he picked up boxers and gray sweatpants on the vanity that he must have placed there before his shower.

He was a hard man, but also comfortable in his skin to be naked and open to showing me what I was missing out on.

He has to know. There was no chance he'd missed the latent desire in my gaze, and it convinced me that he had to be taunting me on purpose. Not reaching out to me but tormenting me with a visual of what I couldn't have.

I came here with a clear mission. I had the goal of speaking as soon as possible, wanting to be completely upfront and honest with him. If I was amenable and cooperative, he had to value that more than when I was stubborn and fighting him. I didn't want to just be an imprisoned hostage here, stuck with no options. Being idle didn't suit me. If I could help, I would.

"I wanted—"

Emily's cries reached me. No matter how new this place was, I was attuned to my daughter. With a sigh, I headed out of his room and went to tend to her before she'd wake up Margie, too.

I hadn't counted on Ivan to follow me. He did, quietly and patiently. Once I picked up a pouty and fussy Emily from the crib Ivan had provided her, he closed the door to her room behind him.

"Sorry."

He huffed a laugh, watching me hold Emily and pace with her, bouncing in my step to calm her. Every time I extended my thumb, bracing my hand on her back, I felt the residual twinge of that cut on my skin from the broken glass. Then the dig of my necklace as Emily reached up and grabbed the thin length, tugging it down against my neck. One of these days, she'd be strong enough to snap it, and I didn't have the money to buy a replacement for the chain. Taking it off wasn't an option, though. I only had this to remember my grandma by.

Emily's cry interrupted me from speaking. Being in her room helped to tame this lust I shouldn't have had for Ivan, too.

"You don't have to apologize for her. She's only a baby."

"A fussy baby."

"Did Margie help?" he asked as he sat in the plush chair across from her crib.

"She did. Thank you."

He dipped his chin in acknowledgment as he watched me.

"Not only did she help with Emily and gave me a chance to nap, but she also…" I walked toward him, reaching into the pocket of my thin robe for my phone. He accepted it, brows raised. "She also helped me record what I could of a call from Steven."

I rattled off Emily's birthdate, the passcode, and he tapped it in. "He called earlier, and I wanted to record it for you to listen to."

Over and over, he played the video I'd hastily thought to record of the call on my phone. Margie texted me the video, and I was glad I had it available for Ivan to listen to. Each time I heard it start over, I cringed internally at the sound in Steven's voice. Cruel. Calculating. Selfish. My anger boiled hot once more at the thought that my father would set up a thug to take Emily like that. To pose her any harm at all.

Ivan listened carefully, narrowing his eyes and not moving as he repeated the short exchange. I didn't interrupt, settling Emily as she clung to my necklace and let me soothe her with walking back and forth.

He set my phone on the small table and regarded me. "What time did he call?"

"The time is in my call log. 4:54."

"What did he say before you recorded?"

I licked my lips, thinking back. "More of the same. Wanting to know where I was. Where you were. I hurried to record it as soon as possible. The ringtone of his call woke me right out of a nap."

He rubbed his chin, looking at the wall before sighing. "What was that about falling in love? What did he mean when he teased you about falling in love with 'this man' too?" Pointing at himself, he raised his brows. "Should I assume he meant me?"

I nodded, then rolled my eyes as another hit of a blush swept over my cheeks. "He said it to get a rise out of me. To taunt me. He always told me that I'd never find a man who would want me."

He watched me closely, adding more suspense to this quiet. I was put on the spot and didn't like it.

"He asked that of you because he seems to know I'm with you. That you captured me. And he thought it would be comical to compare that to the last time I was with a man he knew about—Dominic."

"Has he always been that cruel?"

I nodded. "Cruel? Try evil." Looking up at the ceiling to regain my composure, I turned to pace more for soothing Emily. "For as long as I can remember. No matter the evidence her case had, I am still convinced that he had my mother killed. That it wasn't an accident and that he'd orchestrated it all. My mother was the daughter of his boss on the force, and he didn't like him and how he tried to discipline him at work."

"That's a strong accusation."

I narrowed my eyes at him, feeling this old comfort of anger. "It is. And I stand by it. I mean it when I say there is no lost love for him. He's never cared about me. I've always been a burden on him, foisted off to neglectful babysitters and abusive teachers. Steven was never present, never there. And if he was, it was to belittle me or wonder how I could help him in a scam or stupid ploy to get money."

Ivan leaned forward, resting his elbows on his knees as he peered up at me. "It sounds like you learned your independence early on."

"Not by choice. And I did. I learned everything the hard way because I hated him trying to have any say in what I wanted to do or who I wanted to be friends with. He scared off my boyfriends and persuaded my employers to let him harass me on the clock."

"Scared off your boyfriends?" he asked.

I nodded. "All three of them."

He nodded, pensive for a moment. "What about Dom?"

My spirits sank at the mention of his name.

15

IVAN

She's siding with me. Not Steven. Not the Rossinis.

Becca wanted to stand by me and the Valkov name. By hurrying to record that call, she proved that she wanted me to hear it and learn more about whatever I could use against her father. The urgency that she obeyed, leaving her bed and coming to find me right away, attested to her commitment in her decisions. This wasn't a whim. She wasn't helping me with information as a fluke moment. She was considerate and smart with a kind of quick thinking that I admired.

Becca chose to tell me about that call as soon as she could.

And the ramifications of her decision hit hard. She trusted me. She'd stalwartly refused to give in to any of Steven's demands. He'd asked her over and over to reveal her location, and she held strong against him.

Besides, she didn't know. No one had told Becca where we were, exactly. This Valkov vacation villa was upstate, but there was no way she could've tracked the path here when we'd left the city. She hadn't been blindfolded in the backseat, but her focus had been on Emily, not the scenery passing by.

When Murphy asked where *I* was, she was again ill-equipped with an actual answer. She was napping when I left, unaware that I had taken off, and even if she had been awake, I knew she wouldn't have asked. She wouldn't have taken the risk to be nosy about my affairs. All this time she's been here more like a guest than a hostage, she'd kept to herself and minding Emily. Not once did she inquire about what I did or where I went, intuitively respecting that it wasn't information she needed to know. Maybe she preferred it that way. The less she was aware of, the safer she was in ignorance. I couldn't fault her for that mindset, but I ignored it because considering what she did and didn't know led me to wonder what would happen to her after Murphy was dead.

Still, the realization of her loyalty stunned me. She was loyal to me, not her father or the Rossinis.

Which made it all the more interesting why she was so quick to clam up about my single, pointed question about Dom.

Because something is there between them. A history in the past? A dream for the future? Becca was familiar with Dom. There was no chance in hell she could deny that, and it burned me to understand she had been downplaying her connection to him.

Dmitri showed me the lengthy list of calls she'd had with the most reputable number that we felt was Dominic's. The first assumption that came to mind was that she'd dated him, but she'd rejected that.

Jealousy filled me immediately. It streaked through my veins, lighting up a unique version of rage I'd never experienced before. Women never mattered. They never lasted. I never wanted them to last because I knew every single one of them wouldn't actually want me for who I was, a criminal Mafia man with a preference for hard fucks.

Becca was sneaking further under my skin, though. The mere idea of seeing her filled a dark, twisted corner of my heart. I didn't know how it happened or why. She was supposed to serve the purpose of being here to lure Murphy out. She was not here to make me wonder about love and belonging in the sense of a proper relationship that would endure more than one fling.

But maybe she is doing that, bringing Murphy out of hiding.

The call that she recorded was the first means of communication since we'd made it clear to the criminal world that Becca was captive under the Valkov family. We'd left plenty of messages for Murphy to understand we had his daughter. He hadn't taken the bait yet. He hadn't responded or reacted to any of the news about Becca being held hostage by us.

Until today.

He'd reached out, calling her specifically, and I was damned thankful that she'd recorded it. I already sent the recording from her phone to mine, then shared it with all my brothers and Yusef.

The fucker knew. He knew that we had Becca, but he wasn't interested in negotiating with us. He instead decided to contact her.

As Becca paced with Emily, soothing the teething baby, I mulled over all that his call signified. Murphy was aware that *I* had Becca. Why else would he have asked in that call where I was? The crooked cop knew that she was with me, that Emily was with us too.

I fisted my hand then released my shoulders, wishing that clench would vent out some of my anger. The thought that Murphy had set up Emily's being taken just to interfere with her captivity... It pissed me off to no end. How could any man have the audacity to set up his infant granddaughter to be a token in this war?

He'd tried to use Emily as a way to get to Becca. To me. And I would not stand for that. His call revealed a critical clue that I wouldn't soon forget.

Knowing where Becca was had to be Murphy's attempt to track me. To know where his enemy lurked.

This was all a game of cat and mouse.

And I was fine with that.

I could manage the pressure because Murphy would not win this game. He would not slip away, nor would he harm Emily or Becca ever again.

What I couldn't manage was how Becca went quiet at any mention of Dominic Rossini. It didn't sit well with me how she continued to pace and not answer my question about him. She'd referenced Murphy scaring off boyfriends. Banking on the assumption that

Dominic had been a boyfriend of hers, I wasn't happy with her silence.

She wasn't repeating that silent treatment crap. This was different. Her showing me the recording of that call was the opposite effect of a silent treatment or withholding information.

So, why does she go quiet and look uncomfortable?

I stood, sighing as I left her to handle Emily. Without another word, I left to pour myself a drink in the other room, needing a moment to think without the distraction of her beauty so near. Distance hadn't helped me yet, but I tried to pick through the options of whatever could be at play here. That spike of jealousy wouldn't fade, but when I reentered the room that Emily slept in, I hoped the alcohol would counter my rising temper.

Becca didn't flinch when I returned. She merely carried Emily, swaying slightly like the baby enjoyed. Each move of her hips taunted me, and I wished I could get over this aching desire for her.

"What aren't you telling me about Dom?" I asked, carefully but firmly. I didn't want to enter a shouting match and argue to the point of bothering Emily. I felt bad to "use" the baby as an excuse to ensure a civil conversation, but I'd do whatever was necessary.

"Dominic wasn't a boyfriend, Ivan."

I sipped then shook my head. "Your starting with that disclaimer leads me to believe otherwise." Almost like someone would start with a plea of *Don't get mad, but...*

Her shoulders slumped.

"Start at the beginning."

She turned, walking with Emily. "I first heard of Dominic through someone at school. I never had a chance to go to college. No money. My grades weren't good enough." She shrugged. "To get anywhere in the art crowd, you have to study with the right people and earn a rub-off of their clout. You have to mingle and socialize and rub elbows with other artists or sponsors to even get anyone to know your name. I never had time for that. Since I was sixteen, I've been working one, if not two jobs to put food on the table."

"For Murphy too?"

She rolled her eyes. "He gambled. He owed debts. He operated with favors and still does. Every penny I earned, he saw as his. He'd blow it on drugs or booze. Or try to pay off someone for a better investment. I learned to hide as much as I could so I could simply survive."

She's not kidding about no lost love there.

"I never wanted to give up my dreams, though. My grandmother, my mother's mother, had a studio in the city, and since it was paid for through a friend of hers, the small space was something he couldn't touch. He never wanted it, anyway. So it was there I could keep up with my hobby when I ever had free time. When I went to a gallery opening for a friend, I saw Dominic there. He was curious about my name, saying I looked like someone he knew. He recognized me through Steven, and once I admitted that he was my father, he got very interested in me."

I let her walk and mull in her silence again. It seemed like she was searching for the right words, picking through her memories, and she continued speaking again.

"At first, I was too excited that a rich man like him was even talking to me. He was charming. Knowledgeable about art. Meeting him seemed too good to be true, but I was so enthusiastic for someone—anyone—to pay attention to me and my art. I was suckered instantly. I looked him up that night, and I realized he was an influential, well-off man. I never realized he was in the Mafia. I only looked for his art ties. So, when he offered to sponsor me and show me to galleries in Europe, of course, I said yes."

"You just up and left? Traveled with him?"

I nodded. "I'd just finished my lease for the apartment I had at that time. I was sick of my jobs, and they were dime-a-dozen gigs, anyway. For the first time, I thought why not? Maybe this would be my big break. I traveled with him, like a friend. I always had separate lodgings, and most of the time, I was alone. He had 'business' to do. He was often on the phone or meeting with people. I didn't care. I was just so excited to be in Europe. I saw all the museums. Spent lots of time in galleries. With my sketchbooks, I prepared to make so much artwork, assuming this was it, that I'd be an artist, and not a starving one with a man like Dominic Rossini interested in what I could make."

I rubbed my lip with my finger, watching her open up. "Then what?"

"Then, a few months after I'd been with him, I realized he'd been manipulating me just to keep an eye on what my father was up to."

"Did you ever ask Murphy how or why he knew Dominic?"

She shook her head. "I didn't speak with Steven since I met Dominic. My father had never given a shit about my art. Never will. I didn't want to tarnish my time or association with Dominic by bringing my father into anything. He was so negative, so cruel and dismissive, I wanted to believe that Dominic could almost replace my father's significance in my life. I felt that Dom could be the man who'd look out for me. Who'd want me."

Fisting my hand again, I breathed through the anger filling me at her heartbroken honesty.

"When all he'd done was trick me. He'd conned me into thinking he cared about my artwork, but one night, I overheard him speaking with my father and my eyes were well and truly opened. He and Steven were arguing about a plan."

"A plan for what?"

She shrugged. "No details were shared, probably on purpose. Dom seemed to argue that he thought this plan would be impossible to pull off, but Steven said they had to keep their eye on the long-term goal."

There was my proof. Steven was trying to collaborate with the Rossinis. This wasn't good news for the Bratva, and I was renewed with a sense of putting out the fire before it could take flame.

"I wanted to leave right then and there when I overheard that call. Knowing that Steven could interfere with what I had assumed was a legitimate interest in my artwork was equivalent to my world crashing down." She glanced at me, sadder yet. "I had this gut instinct, you know? I just *knew* something fishy was going on, and I didn't want any part of it."

"Did you leave?"

She nodded. "I told Dominic that I wanted to go home. That I overheard him and I refused to be associated with anything my father was involved in, that I didn't trust him, and therefore, I didn't trust Dominic either. He didn't take the confrontation well. It was stupid, from an amateur artist's perspective, to ever talk back to a prospective sponsor. But he didn't even mention my art. He admitted that he only ever approached me as insurance to keep a closer eye on my father, that while I was with Dominic, Steven would have to behave."

Just like I'm doing with you. She had been a pawn before, but I hated to think I wasn't any better. Against my judgment, I was falling for her in a way I never had for a woman.

"He scowled and lashed out, telling me he was sick of me, anyway. Sick of pretending that my artwork was good. Sick of spending so much energy to keep an eye on a man who only lied and played games. So sick of me that..." She sniffled, tipping her chin up defiantly. "That he raped me that night before I flew home."

I tensed. Clenching my fists tight and bracing my legs to stand, I stared at her. "He raped you?"

She nodded, unafraid to look me in the eye now. Almost as though she challenged me to judge her.

"Is Emily the product of that rape?"

Once more, she nodded, but this time, shame filled her eyes as she turned to look away.

16

BECCA

I couldn't bear the look in Ivan's eyes. He was so tense, but I couldn't pinpoint why.

At first, I wondered if he could've been upset that I trespassed into his room and dared to stand there in his privacy while he finished his shower. I'd been too stunned to move then, tantalized by his naked form.

Then once I shared that recorded call with him, I worried that he would react in anger near Emily. I hadn't felt danger around Ivan since I'd come here, but he had been so upset, so riled up at the sound of Steven's voice that I couldn't help but want to cringe.

Now, as I elaborated about how Dominic had used me, he looked furious. Ferally angry.

I warred between two options. Shut up and go to bed or try to explain further. I wasn't hiding anything else, but something in the way he stared at me suggested that he thought I was still untrustworthy.

Even after I'd shared that call with him. If that couldn't be the biggest sign of surrendering to him and his plans, I wasn't sure what else I could do.

"I thought you said you had no connection with Dominic."

I swallowed, rubbing my hand down Emily's back both to soothe her and seek my own comfort from her.

"I don't. He sent me packing after he raped me."

"You share a child with him."

I refused to flinch at his hard tone. "I don't share her with him. He doesn't even know she exists."

He arched one brow. "Are you sure about that?"

I nodded, but that gesture now felt like a lie. So many things convinced me that Steven was the one trying to use Emily to get to me, but I felt certain that Dominic didn't know about Emily. Nor that he would care.

Unless he wanted to use Emily as a way to get to Steven? I dismissed that thought. That would only work if Steven cared about her, and he didn't. He didn't care about me, either.

It was such a sad mess. And I was supposed to call it my life.

"I was no one to Dom," I insisted, knowing that Ivan wouldn't leave any of this alone. He wanted to know the full story, and I wouldn't accomplish anything by not sharing since I was already in this deep.

"Except a way to keep tabs on Murphy."

I nodded. "That was the *only* value he saw in stringing me along. And he did. That was all Dom did from the first moment I spoke with him. He saw me as someone to use for a bigger purpose, and because he was so charming and involved in the art world, I was the ideal idiot to fall for everything he said or suggested."

I hated to revisit the gullible moments I would never be able to take back. All those times when I was a naïve, stupid woman with tunnel vision on my goal of becoming a successful artist one day.

"Dom blindsided me the night I said I wanted to leave, that night I overheard him arguing with Steven. But all along, during those several months when he tried to con me into thinking and believing that he'd be the person to nudge me into recognition as an artist anywhere, he'd been manipulating me. Lying. Teasing. He'd led me to think my passion wasn't silly, but I had a chance of being a real career artist. It was *how* he twisted my mind, playing with my heart."

He tilted his head to the side. "You loved him?"

"Never. Not even close. But I loved my art. And he'd hit me and tricked me where it hurt most."

All that mental warfare stung with an agonizing depth that I doubted anyone could understand, much less sympathize with. Least of all, Ivan.

He watched me, stoic and cool with his expression, and I felt desperate to know what he was thinking. During these weeks as his hostage, as a guest at this fancy house, he'd come to matter. I didn't see him all the time. It wasn't a nonstop companionship or control. I'd begun to wonder if he was trying to maintain his distance from a woman and her baby until that evening I cut my hand. I couldn't make sense of what was happening between me and Ivan, but it didn't feel like a hostage situation.

It felt like something that could deepen, especially with my offer of trust when I recorded that call for him.

I wanted to be delusional and think we could be... friends.

His icy demeanor with this tale of my darkest moment had me thinking that was a foolish wish.

Ivan was a hard man. I saw it in his scarred body used to brutality, both delivered by his hands and whoever had inflicted all those scars on him.

He could be aloof, remaining in charge no matter what and always calling the shots as the superior in any troublesome situation.

As I glanced at him again, I wanted to believe that he looked so stony and mad because he was upset *for* me, not at me. But having to wonder about that should have explained that I had no business wanting him at all.

I knew Ivan was a rough man. He'd played with me so expertly. He'd taken me so roughly and quickly that I should've been stuck in this déjà vu sensation of being raped again. He hadn't sought my verbal consent, but he hadn't raped me. I'd been so aroused and confused. I *wanted* him, and after I'd calmed from the rush of that orgasm I still hadn't forgotten from weeks ago, I understood how much I preferred his kind of blunt and harsh treatment. I preferred the way he didn't lie and try to use psychological warfare against me.

"He tricked me," I repeated, needing him to understand that fact.

I hadn't been a willing participant in any of this danger. I never once volunteered for these cards to be dealt to me.

And just the same, I felt confident about Ivan, no matter how much I was coming to yearn for his touch.

He'd made himself clear, painfully so. From that first time he saw me at that sex club, he'd been honest. I served him a purpose, as bait, and that was the only reason he wanted me around. I was nothing but a piece to move around in this war.

I wasn't a woman he'd want or lust for.

Sometimes, the truth hurt as bad as the lies. It was at this moment that I realized how badly my craving for him and his touch had become.

I sighed, catching him eyeing Emily. Every time I saw her in his arms, he disarmed me that much more. When he picked her up and calmed her down, so unerringly good at that, he proved his patience for her, his regard for her comfort.

Those moments felt like lies. Like contradictions when he seemed like daddy material, tender and sweet, while at the same time I recognized him for who he really was—a violent criminal, a Mafia man.

"She's a Rossini," he said. It sounded not like a question but a statement. A reiteration of what I'd painfully explained.

"Yes." I narrowed my eyes, wondering if he was doubting me. "I didn't—I don't—sleep around. There wasn't anyone else, and the timing of her conception matched when I tested positive."

He lifted his hand, almost seeming annoyed as he cut me off. "I wasn't implying anything else."

"Hard not to think that with the way you're reacting." I huffed.

"Emily is the daughter of the Valkovs' enemy," he added, as though he had to spell it out for me.

"And I'm the daughter of the crooked cop you want to kill, another enemy," I bit back.

He stood, regarding Emily as she slept against my chest. Still, I swayed in place, not wanting to rouse her to fuss while I railed against the pain in my heart.

"You are." He looked me up and down. "And I won't forget it."

Without giving me a chance to reply, he turned and left me in the room with my sleeping daughter. His parting glance sickened me.

He'd looked at Emily with something like disdain, like he viewed her as a bastard child, not an innocent baby who was getting good at capturing his attention.

Even worse was his regard for me—a tight smirk as though he wouldn't be deterred from squeezing out every drop of usefulness out of me, the daughter of his nemesis he was determined to kill.

He shut the door after himself, and the soft close sounded so final, so judgmental. After sharing my hardest story with him, all he wanted to do was shut *me* out. And I hated how badly it hurt.

17

IVAN

When Becca confided in me about Dominic being Emily's father, I felt threatened. That my enemy, a dangerous man from the Italian Mob, could have a bigger impact on Emily than I could. It didn't calm me to know that Dominic wasn't aware of Emily's birth or that he'd impregnated Becca.

What really got to me was the fact that he'd raped her. That he'd taken her against her will, with contempt, and kicked her out of his life.

I fucked her too, and I bet some would claim I'd done the same thing, that I'd raped her. But she'd wanted it. And still did. I didn't miss the longing in her eyes. Like when she gazed at me after I stepped out of the shower.

Now, I had to add Dominic fucking Rossini to my already long kill list. That asshole would never have a moment of peace or safety as long as he lived. To hurt Becca, to harm her, to violate her with only the intention of malice and pain…

It was an unforgivable crime.

He would pay. I would make sure of it, but I had to figure out how and where. When, too. Alek ordered me to handle Murphy. We had to get that corrupt officer out of the way before he tried to attack the Bratva or bring our organization down. He was a direct threat to us.

The Rossinis weren't as big of a danger at the present. With their record for infighting and skewed business interests, they didn't pose an immediate danger to us.

But Dominic Rossini had earned a death sentence. Knowing that he'd raped Becca and manipulated her...

It was personal now. As soon as I took care of Murphy, Dominic was next.

Unless I can kill two birds with one stone.

I still didn't know what Murphy and the Rossinis were plotting together, or if they even were after all this time since Becca heard that call between her father and Dominic, but I had to assume something was up.

Despite the desire to reach for Becca and pull her into my arms, I took the easier way out and left her in Emily's room. I yearned to hug that woman and tell her that I would see justice for how she'd become a mother. I wanted to be a hero for her and explain that she didn't have to worry about Dom being in her life at all anymore.

Looking at the mother and daughter together was just too hard. It pained me to see them, strong yet alone. Abandoned but having each other. Becca and Emily looked so good and pure together, full of love that would never cease or fade under any condition.

They resembled the perfect picture of a future I'd never considered. A wife and a child to hold and protect. A woman to love and cherish with a daughter to raise and enjoy.

Once more, as I woke up the next morning, still bothered by how tempting that woman was, I wondered if my brothers were getting to me.

I'd left her last night because of how badly I wanted to comfort her. It seemed like such a vulnerability, to express sorrow and regret on her behalf that she'd ever suffered.

This morning, I felt prickly at the possibility that I was threatened by what she seemed to offer, something I never thought I could have or find.

Alek started it all, marrying Mila. Then Nik and Amy. One by one, the Valkov brothers were falling for women. I didn't think any less of Alek or Nik. They weren't weaker men for finding their other halves.

But I'd given up the hope that I would find love too. That I would *want* to find love.

Once I got up and started my day, I let the simmering anger about Becca being raped guide me to action.

I didn't see her in the house. She and Margie preoccupied Emily while the women cooked and talked in the kitchen. With Becca busy, I slipped out of the house and did my best to stay focused on my job.

Checking in with Yusef and the others yielded nothing promising. Then a meeting with my brothers, where we discussed this call that Becca recorded, took several hours of my day.

"She really must not give a shit what happens to him, then," Alek mused once we'd talked about the call at the mansion.

Just like I had last night, I felt on edge about being in the city and away from Becca. This distance gnawed at me. It wasn't helping. It wasn't making me give up on wanting her. It only goaded me to miss her harder.

How the hell did she get under my skin so fast, so deep?

"She says there is no lost love," I told them.

"I can see that." Nik nodded, peering at me. "But is she finding it with *you?*"

I knew they'd make a big deal out of Murphy taunting Becca in that call.

"He was just trying to get a rise out of her," I argued, shaking my head.

"So, nothing's... happening?" Dmitri asked with a knowing smirk.

I glowered at him.

"Wait. *Ivan?*" Maxim snorted. "He's next to get a woman?"

"No." I sat up straighter, hating this teasing. "I'm not. She's a hostage. Not my woman."

"You seem possessive," Dmitri added.

"That's just the kind of person Ivan is," Alek said, almost flippantly, as though he wanted to move past all this awkward talk.

"And it doesn't fucking matter anyway." I rubbed my face, aggravated. "I do want to put more men on Dominic Rossini. He's signed his death warrant for raping her."

Maxim laughed once. "Sure, you don't have *any* feelings for your 'hostage' now."

"Shut the fuck up," I warned our youngest brother.

"But first, Murphy," Alek reminded.

He wouldn't care if I wanted to seek revenge with Dom for raping Becca. It was one more enemy we wouldn't have to deal with.

"First, Murphy," I agreed.

"No luck on tracing it," Dmitri said. "But I'm going to have someone install a program to record her calls. It's... uh, nice that she wanted to go that extra step and record it. I modified her phone to track it, but since it's an older model, it's not as easy to record calls."

"She wants to help us," I said, confident that I wasn't lying about it. Becca hadn't given any impression that she cared about Murphy, and after the man admitted to setting Emily up to be taken, I doubted she'd ever care about her father again.

Instead of going back to the house, I sought another distraction. Seeing Becca with Emily was too much of a temptation to resist. Being at the vacation villa made it too easy for me to approach her, and after last night, I had no clue how I would do that.

Sticking to my responsibilities as a Valkov brother, I headed to another club. LeVant's would be fine. Kenneth was supervising there, but that didn't necessarily mean all the sex clubs could run smoothly without my efforts.

As I walked into another club, letting the darkness of the place calm me, the familiar sounds and smells welcoming me into the familiar atmosphere of sex and thrills, I hoped that being here could help me shake off some of this funkiness, to let go of some steam.

No other woman tempted me. I found nothing alluring here, but I wasn't trying. My main role was to keep an eye on things, and as I tried my damnedest not to obsess and think about Becca, I strained to focus here.

None of my brothers wanted the responsibilities of these clubs, and it wasn't a fickle task. I'd employed competent staff to run things, but someone had to be in charge, and that was me.

Before I made a complete circuit and checked everything in the club, I spotted a familiar face.

We were just talking about her. My conversation with Kenneth at LeVant's seemed like days ago, but it was only last night that he'd mentioned Veronica. I hadn't forgotten how he'd warned me that she was on the lookout for me at LeVant's.

And here she was in the flesh—mostly bare flesh with only a thong on. Her dyed black hair was thinning but intricately braided, all the better to be pulled on, she'd insisted in the past.

The second I entered this corner of the club, she spotted me. Kenneth hadn't been lying about her interest in seeing me. She'd asked around about me already, and now that we were both here, she lit up with a smile and beelined for me.

No. Not tonight. Not... ever. I didn't want a quick, gritty fuck with her. I wanted Becca no matter how hard I tried to tell myself otherwise.

"Ivan," she purred in a greeting, coming close but not to hug me. Some people used stupid nicknames and aliases here, but I was only ever myself—available and ready to fuck hard. Or I used to be. She hadn't forgotten that I disliked hugs and preferred to keep my distance, and I appreciated that she didn't try to pull a stunt like hugging me or kissing my cheek as she was wont to do with others.

"Veronica." I nodded at her in greeting. "Having a good night?" My role wasn't one of providing customer service, but I had nothing to gain from avoiding manners with her.

"Now I am." She eyed me seriously.

I shook my head. "No."

I wasn't interested. At all. Not with her. Not only was she too wild to trust, but she also wasn't Becca.

"Oh, don't be a prude." She smiled saucily, almost too quickly that it didn't reach her eyes. "My new husband is such a bore. He suggested that I pay triple for getting a room with the man of my choice tonight."

I shook my head again. Money was nice, but not tonight.

"And I want you."

"Too bad." Others could fit her bill.

The only woman I wanted was hours away, safe with her daughter under the Bratva's care.

"I won't take no for an answer." Veronica smiled again, but this one was even weaker. Like she was forcing it.

"I can find you someone else to—"

"I want *you*, Ivan." Now she broke protocol, gripping my shirt sleeve.

I was a dominant motherfucker, sexually and otherwise. No one told me what to do. No one tried to get their way with me. Veronica knew that. She was no green girl or newcomer to this scene.

For her to touch me anyway, something was up.

I looked at her closer, noticing the tells that she wasn't behaving like she usually did. I picked up on the hint of impatience and urgency in her eyes. The fear in the tense lines on her brow and the tension of her jaw as she forced that smile not to fall from her face.

"Veronica, I don't think so."

"No. I *need* to see you. I have to."

I narrowed my eyes, unable to shake the suspicion that she sounded desperate and almost afraid.

"Please," she added, dragging her finger down her bare chest. Her tits didn't move much as she stepped closer, pressing herself against my side. Mostly plastic and all fake, Veronica looked like a woman half my age. Surgery and cosmetic assistance went a long way.

"Please. Let's get a room. Huh?" She reached up, stroking her hand over my shirt and stopping at my waistband. Tugging me to face her, she held on close.

I kept my hands to the side, not touching her or encouraging her at all. While I stared down at her, my irritation faded.

She put on a good act, but I was sharp. I caught the fear in her eyes at the chance I'd say no. I noticed how she glanced around the room nervously, as though she feared being caught.

It wasn't about *me*. She didn't seem hellbent on getting me in a room for something filthy, rotten, and sexual.

But she had something to say.

If she was fucking with me, I would be angry. But the terror and nervousness in her eyes didn't lie. This woman was good at trying to get her way sexually and topping from the bottom, but I felt like she was trying to tell me something that she didn't want anyone else to know about.

Her lithe form pressed against me, her breasts rubbing over my arm.

All I could think about was how badly I wished Becca could approach me like this. Confident in her desire for me. Determined to have her wicked way with me in a place of sex and excitement like this.

I thought back to how I'd met her, how I'd found her so bewildered and alarmed, yet intrigued at the club when I'd arranged for her to fall into my hands with that delivery.

Becca was too good to ever want to come to a club like this. She was too innocent and wary to ever approach me with seduction as her intention.

I wanted that redheaded beauty to be here, eager for me to tie her up again and take her sweet pussy hard.

But it wouldn't happen. We were too different, and that alone should've been a reminder that we'd never work. That she'd never succumb to a hard life like mine and *want* me.

"Hmm?" Veronica asked, pawing at me.

Her touch and presence didn't interest me. She did jar me from the wishes to have Becca here, and I was motivated to do whatever was necessary to get back on the road and see her. Even if I wouldn't act on my desire for her, I was a glutton for punishment to want to be near her in that vacation villa, to feel peaceful with the fact that she was safe and close by.

"All right." I narrowed my eyes at Veronica. I had no intention of playing with her or anyone else in this place, but the sooner I heard her out and asked her what the hell she wanted from me, the faster I could return to the woman I wanted and couldn't have.

18

BECCA

I was disappointed but not surprised when I didn't see Ivan the next day. He'd left me so suddenly in Emily's room that I could only assume he judged me for having the baby of his enemy.

Or maybe he thought less of me for "letting" myself get raped. I was the victim in this, but who knew? Maybe from his perspective, I was an idiot to ever get involved with Dom to be in the position of his raping me.

I didn't have that perspective about it, but Ivan's abrupt departure from the room was telling. *Something* bothered him to walk away like that, without a single response to what I shared. I wasn't deluding myself to think he'd react with overwhelming sympathy. He was a hard man who lived a hard life. But still, he could have at least tossed a *damn, that sucks* remark to ease the sting of bringing up the difficult topic.

All I got was avoidance. He was, again, busy with something for the Bratva. However, I wasn't alone. Margie was a blessing, and while I couldn't get over how good she was with Emily, entertaining her as she showed me a recipe for cookies that she swore would brighten any gloomy day, I debated asking her for advice.

I didn't want to tell her about how I was raped either. That wasn't a story to broadcast all over the place, and likely not appropriate to tell a virtual stranger, the hired help who'd just shown up.

She beckoned me to *want* to speak up. I had no girlfriends to count on for advice. My mother had died too soon, probably due to Steven's plans. My grandmother was the only semblance of female companionship, and she'd passed too soon as well. At work—the courier job I was no doubt fired from upon my first no-call, no-show—I had coworkers to do small talk with, but no confidants. No friends.

"This rainy weather isn't all that's dragging you down today, is it?" Margie asked as we stirred the dough. Two batches were her goal. We'd have one here for ourselves and the guards, then more to have Ivan bring to his brothers in the city the next time he went.

I didn't know much about Mafia organizations, and it seemed silly that they could be normal people who enjoyed a basic treat like homemade cookies.

"What do you mean?" I blew out a breath to send my hair flying up and out of my vision.

"You seem upset."

I shrugged, glad Emily was napping so I could have an adult conversation. "I don't like being idle."

She smiled. "Well, good thing we have this task of baking cookies. Do you miss your job?"

I shook my head. "No. Not really. It was just a dime-a-dozen thing that never would have ended up in a higher pay."

"Family, then?"

I bit my lip, considering what to tell her. She was in deep with the family, but I wasn't sure if she knew what Ivan was doing. I had a hunch she was ever present in their lives but didn't involve herself with *what* they did.

"Well, Ivan's hoping to kill my father, who likely arranged for my mother's death. And my grandmother passed away years ago."

She nodded, somber. "Is she the one who made that?" Her spatula pointed at my necklace. "I notice you like to touch the pendant often."

I did then, smiling. "Yes. It's special to me, all I have to remember her by."

"It's beautiful." She leaned in to see it closer as I held it up, but as I lifted it, the chain snapped. "Oh, crap. Emily's been tugging on it so often. I knew that would happen sooner or later."

"Oh, no worries," Margie said as I set the necklace on the window ledge. "I have a spare chain in my bag. I don't use it. I think it's gold, not silver, but it's yours if you'd like."

"Thanks." She was too sweet.

"I'll grab it after these are in the oven."

"She was my inspiration to become an artist."

"Oh! That's fantastic."

Is it? If I hadn't been so eager to pursue a career in the arts, I never would've met Dom.

But then I never would've had Emily, either. She was my heart and joy. I didn't ever consider being raped a blessing, but my baby certainly was.

"It'll be nice then when Ivan can bring you to the house with the others."

I frowned. "The others?"

"Mila and Amy." Margie smiled wider. "And I'm sure they'll bombard you with questions, seeing as you've already had a baby."

I wasn't following. "Who are they?"

"Alek's and Nik's wives. They're both expecting."

"Oh." I blinked, shaking my head at her presumption. "But I'm not... I'm just..." I laughed once. "I'm a hostage here. Not *with* Ivan like that or anything."

"Maybe for now," she teased lightheartedly.

"For good." I couldn't shake the horrible feeling of his just walking away from me last night after that raw and exposing story I told him.

"Nonsense. I called it with Mila. And I predicted it with Amy." She turned to wink at me. "I've got a motherly intuition about those boys. I've seen the way Ivan looks at you. And Emily."

"And how's that?" *He could barely face me last night when I told him I'd carried Dom's baby.*

"Like he's one inch away from being besotted."

I laughed harder. "Yeah, *right.*"

129

"You don't think so?"

"No. I know so. I realize I haven't known Ivan for long, but I highly doubt he'll ever look at me as anything but as his hostage. For the purpose of killing my father."

Each time I thought about it, it seemed so surreal. It was almost like I was looking forward to Steven's death, and how messed up was that?

He'd always been a nuisance in my life, the instigator of nothing but asking *favors*. I'd never wished anyone dead, but the second he admitted that he'd arranged for someone to take Emily, he was firmly on my shit list.

Fortunately, Margie understood that I didn't want to talk about Ivan and her fanciful ideas that he and I could be together. I wouldn't be joining the ranks of the other Valkov wives, even though it sounded like it would be nice to be included like that. I'd always wanted a sister, and having sisters-in-law would be a blessing.

Just one I'll never have.

After the cookies were baked and we tasted a couple, she left me to my own devices while she did laundry.

I was too rested to nap, and I didn't have much to do to tidy up, so I took advantage of Emily's quiet and grabbed a notebook from the study. Even though the pages were lined, it was an ideal source to sketch and draw. Sculptures were my favorite medium, but something about the abundant light in this place called to me.

Seated near the huge windows that opened out to the gardens out back, I set the tip of the pencil to the paper and drew. Doodled and sketched. A few versions of landscapes filled the pages, but then I switched to more abstract images. Then rough ideas of sculptures.

I couldn't remember the last time I'd had the freedom to just sit and be. To think and draw. To create.

Grateful to Ivan for this chance to relax and draw, I got into it, producing many pages of plans and ideas—most of which I doubted I'd ever have a chance to see to fulfillment. It'd been months since I last went to my studio, and I knew better than to hope to go there until Murphy showed up and "freed" me from being a hostage.

I wasn't in any hurry to leave, and that was a startling concept to accept. I was happy here. Pampered. Not facing undue stress and the workaholic rate of being a single mother without many prospects.

Ivan treated me well out here, even if he couldn't stand to be near me, and I wished that I could stay.

Later that evening, as I prepared Emily for bedtime, I snuggled with her on the bed and watched her eyes droop shut. Letting her rest with me in the bed never turned out well. I was always too afraid I'd roll over her. Sometimes I needed her company, though, to see that she was healthy and well as proof that I was doing the best I could by her.

Stroking my finger over her cheek, I sighed and wondered what would be next for her, too.

If Ivan let us go without any trauma, I'd need to find another job. He'd told me that my apartment would be paid for until I was "released" and that meant I had a place to go home to, but I'd need to job hunt. Then Hannah. What would I do for a sitter? I hoped she was all right, but I couldn't dare ask her to be the sitter again.

As I envisioned a life after being here with Ivan, confident that I would remain unharmed since I had been all this time, I despised having to leave at all.

Being near Ivan felt right. Hearing Margie assume I'd be another woman to fit in with Mila and Amy sounded perfect.

I wished, from the depths of my heart, that things could be different. Just like I couldn't regret Dominic raping me because it gave me Emily, I refused to hold a grudge against Ivan for capturing me and holding me hostage here. Without his doing that, I never would have had a chance to know that bliss of him fucking me hard. I never would have had an opportunity to slightly get to know him—enough that I missed him when he was gone.

"I wish I could give you everything you deserve," I whispered to Emily as she slept.

A big, safe home with room for her to play to her little heart's content instead of being cramped in my dated, chilly apartment. Her own room, without any bright lights from the street shining through the curtains. Brand-new clothes instead of threadbare thrifted items. Food without any worries that it'd run out.

All of it. Ivan had done this for me, for her, without a single hesitation, and I appreciated it.

More than anything, I wished I could let her continue this slow and tenuous bonding experience I'd witnessed between them. How he gazed at her when he held her when I wasn't available to take over. How she peered at him with wonder and batted her hands at his face as she babbled.

I appreciated all he'd done, but the depth of my longing and desire for him didn't stop there. Still, after all these weeks, I felt the phantom tingle of his cock filling me so harshly. That delicious thrill of surrendering to him as he teased me then made me come so hard. The touch of his hands on me, free to do as he pleased while he kept me tied up, and that was the kicker. I knew that he wouldn't hurt me for the hell of it. He'd understood, without any words or cues given to him, how to push me so far that I'd stop dwelling in the thoughts clouding my head and just *feel*. To just let go. That liberation was amazing, something I knew he would be the only master of, and it filled me with desolation that no other man would ever compare.

It was all too easy to wish for a life *with* him. Ivan was a rugged, rough man, but it was too damn simple to see how he could fit in with us. As my expert lover. As Emily's patient daddy. As our formidable protector.

I blinked, overwhelmed with wanting him and missing him. This realization of love had snuck up on me, but I knew without a doubt that I was falling for him.

I was catching feelings for the man I had no business desiring at all.

19

IVAN

Veronica chose a room and I followed her into it. The fact that she didn't want to have a scene with a window where people could watch wasn't the norm. She really did want privacy with me, and I worried that this seclusion with me—that she'd never sought before because she liked to put on a show—meant that she wanted me exclusively.

I wasn't available.

I really wasn't. My body craved Becca's. My dick wanted to sink into her pussy. And it was that sweet young woman's voice I wanted to hear moaning my name.

No one else, especially not Veronica.

"You're not..." The older woman turned to me after I closed the door. "Lock it."

I arched my brow, reaching back to flip the lever for the lock. Our clubs didn't allow total lock-downs for the safety of the clients. Staff could override the locks anyone on the inside implemented, but she wanted that extra precaution.

Just what the hell do you want here?

"You're not wired or anything, are you?"

I crossed my arms. I was intrigued and slightly annoyed, but now, I was curious and bordering on full-out concern. "What the fuck are you talking about?"

She licked her lips. Her pale face was pink in here, lit with the glow of only a red lamp in the corner. I walked over toward the wall and turned on the bigger light near the softer cushioned area designed for aftercare. Now, I saw her fully, and the fear and worry on her face were unmistakable.

"You're not wired, right? Listening devices and such?"

I shook my head. "No. I'm not."

"Because I don't want it coming back to me that I told anyone about this."

"Told anyone what?" I was on edge, alert and impatient.

"I was drugged."

I narrowed my eyes, waiting for more.

"Not here." She licked her lips again and stepped closer while lowering her voice. "Not at your family's clubs. But at another place."

I shrugged. "And?" That was the nature of what happened when someone played in places like this with the people who liked to come here.

"It was either at the place uptown with the triple code check to enter or that newer little club closer to the river."

I knew which ones she meant. That triple-check place was something we'd recently sold to another company, no longer wanting the high costs of running a club in that area. We'd never made enough profit to keep it going there. The small and new place by the river had only been open for a few months. It paid for me to keep abreast of the competition out there, and it had been my suggestion to Alek to sell that club uptown.

"Okay..."

"And it was bad, Ivan. Bad." She gripped her fingers together and wrung them. For the first time in the years that she'd been a regular in these kinky crowds, she looked her age. Feeble, scared, and weak. Most of all, worried.

"What about it?"

She shook her head. "I've been roofied before. I've asked to be drugged up. All kinds of things. You know. You know how I like to push the limits and be extreme."

I nodded.

"And I've done a lot of stupid shit in my life. Back when I was younger, younger than you are now, I did it all. Crack, LSD, hell, *everything* on the market, Ivan. I've lived a wild life."

"Then what's wrong now?" *Why the hell are you telling* me *about it?*

She swallowed. "It was bad. I'm telling you. I've never taken anything that messed me up like that. I was life-flighted. I died three times on the way there."

"Fuck."

"Whatever they gave me was not some simple recreational pill, all right? It's some bad shit."

"But you didn't get it here?"

She shook her head. "No. But something is going on, Ivan. I'm ninety percent certain it was something I was given at that place uptown. That you used to run."

I narrowed my eyes, wondering if this was something I needed to worry about.

"It was *bad*, Ivan. And I just thought you might know something about what's going around and all. Because that shit can kill."

Thinking back to the concern about the pair of young women who were intoxicated at LeVant's, I considered the possibility of this being a pattern. If these stronger, different drugs had been used at LeVant's, then that wasn't good for us. We didn't want bad product there. And we didn't want anyone thinking that the Bratva-operated sex clubs were places to avoid.

You're older, though. Veronica wasn't a youthful woman like the two Kenneth had seen at LeVant's. Then again, Veronica was nimble and fit, disguising her age with a toned body.

"I hate that you had to deal with this," I said sincerely, "but that place is under new management. New owners. If they're pushing shady shit, that's not associated with me, with the Valkov name."

She shrugged, shaking her head as she looked away, clearly

uncomfortable. "Technically, yeah. It isn't one of your clubs anymore, but what if that crap was going around when it was?"

I wouldn't have any way of knowing. Clients stayed loyal to clubs. Even though the Bratva no longer operated it, some people might not realize it yet. We checked everyone who came inside the doors. Security was tight, but things slipped through. It happened.

Is someone setting up the Bratva to take this hit? Planting drugs on our turf and making us look bad?

We had too many enemies to single anyone out. And it was a fine-lined dilemma. We pushed drugs. We sold all kinds of product, but nothing out of the norm, nothing that couldn't already be obtained elsewhere. Peddling crap that killed wouldn't help us at all, and I tried to consider what we'd be facing if someone were coming after the Bratva like that.

"Thanks for telling me," I said, reaching out to set my hand on her shoulder.

"Yeah. Sure."

Damn, she was really off-kilter about this. All that seductive and sultry attitude out on the floor was just a ploy to convince me into this room alone.

"Just, you know. Don't tell anyone I told you about this. All right? With my age, I don't want anyone getting the wrong idea. That I'm too old to handle this kind of life. Like I'm not cut out for a good time anymore."

I huffed and rolled my eyes. "Veronica, you'll be fucking someone all the way to the grave."

She smiled and lifted her brows slightly. It was the first slip of humor since she'd spoken in here.

"I won't rat you out. I appreciate your telling me."

We exited, and I didn't waste another minute to leave. On the drive back to Becca out of the city, I called Alek and brought him up to speed.

"You think it's lousy timing?" he asked once I'd told him everything.

"Maybe. If this was happening when we still owned that club, then it'd be a bigger issue."

He cleared his throat. "True, but you said something happened at LeVant's. No, Maxim told me."

"Those women seemed fine."

"It might not be a bad idea to put more security at the clubs. Screen the guests more."

I frowned as I drove. "Only if it doesn't scare off the clientele." The last thing we needed was for everyone to think something was wrong and that we were being suspicious at a location where security and confidentiality were expected.

"Yeah." He sighed. "I know what you mean. And I know you're out a lot, busy with Becca."

I narrowed my eyes. "Not *with* her."

"Well, you're busy with trying to take Murphy out."

Except, he was right. I was busy with Becca. She was on my mind constantly. "Are you giving me shit for personally watching over her at that vacation villa?"

"Maybe I am. You don't have to be out there."

I bit my lip, opting for silence.

"But I respect that maybe you *want* to be."

"It's not like that."

"What is it like, then?"

I opened and closed my mouth.

"You moved Margie out there to help Becca with her kid."

"Because she was sick and needed a break and—" I cut myself off, hearing how defensive I was.

He chuckled. "It's fine, man. It's fine. Happens to all of us."

"Nothing's happening to me."

"Sure. Look, I'm not going to get into your business. All I need to know is that you can still handle what I've asked of you. If you start to have feelings for Becca, will you be able to kill her father?"

I nodded even though he couldn't see it. "Yes. Absolutely."

"Even if it might hurt her."

I snorted. "I'm starting to think that Becca and Emily are at more risk of being hurt the longer he lives."

We disconnected the call, and I tried to resist the anxious feeling that came with making that comment. Murphy was a risk to Emily. He'd set her up to be taken. And he had always been a danger to Becca, never caring for her and asking her to do favors when she was just an ignorant innocent.

Murphy was still trying to use her. He wanted to know where she was to track me, for starters. But what else that man wanted with her, I didn't know. And it bothered me to no end that I couldn't stop this thought that I was missing something.

When I arrived at the villa, checking on Emily, then Becca, as was my habit, I felt calmer.

I wouldn't let anyone get to them. Being here felt right, and I knew that Alek was correct in some of his guesses.

My feelings about this naïve young woman weren't the same as they were when I took her from her old life. I cared. I worried. And I was starting to get obsessed with their being in my life.

Which was why I had no scruples about ensuring I would be one step ahead of Murphy if he tried to separate Becca from me, if he tried to distance us so she would no longer be a lure for him to reveal himself.

The house was guarded. The men here wouldn't fail me.

But those reassurances weren't enough. They didn't stop me from reaching for that necklace she always wore. Careful not to wake her, I pressed a tiny tab to the top line of the pendant. Having my fingers so close to her flesh was torture. I wanted to reach out and feel her warmth again.

Instead, I let the pendant rest on her flesh again, delicately so as not to wake her.

Then I stepped back, gazing at her and marveling that our paths had ever crossed.

And how intertwined they'd become.

Most of all, how I intended to keep her safe and with me for as long as possible.

20

BECCA

Ivan wasn't home.

I rolled my eyes as I changed Emily's post-nap diaper.

This wasn't *home*. Not for him. Not for me or Emily, but for the lack of knowing what else to call this enormous party house, it was the first word that came to mind.

I'd dreamed about him last night. It was such a potent figment of my imagination that I could have sworn I smelled him too. And I wondered how long it would last.

Would he avoid me until Steven was dead?

Did he need more time to maintain his distance from me until he could come to terms with the fact that Emily was the child of Dominic Rossini?

Or was it something else altogether? I'd only had a couple of boyfriends. I never had time to date. Maybe it was something I wasn't aware of. Some cue that I was missing as a much younger woman with an older, more experienced man.

And the experience he *has...*

I sighed, helping Emily up and carrying her out of her room to find Margie.

Ivan had tons of experience to have cultured his air of dominance.

He'd no doubt slept around managing sex clubs like that place where he'd set me up to deliver what was likely a placebo of a package to him.

Maybe he finds me lacking.

I hated to analyze and second-guess myself, but I was desperate for an answer. A reason. He'd come with me that one time. He'd cared enough to massage my wrists. He hadn't raped me. He'd fucked me hard, but after that, he stopped making any advances.

And I wanted him to. In the absence of any time spent with him anymore, I latched on to a second chance at sex with him. With the tenacity of a fever dream, Ivan was who I fantasized about in my waking hours and who I envisioned in my sleep.

Maybe it was that bad for him.

I knew I wasn't what he was used to. I'd never... played with someone or let someone insert anything in me. I was so vanilla that I didn't even own a vibrator or any other sex toy.

Maybe I'm too different, too innocent and sheltered sexually for him to want me again.

"There she is!" Margie beamed at us as we entered the kitchen. The high chair was already set up for Emily's lunch. She waved her hands and babbled in excitement.

Laughing lightly, I set her in the chair and moved to the table for the salad and fruit dish Margie had arranged. I was pleased to see she'd set a plate for herself too. I could use her company to stay out of my head.

All these thoughts and wishes about Ivan had to simmer down somehow.

"I saw your notebook," she said as she wheeled Emily closer to the table, before she took her seat.

I smiled at the book I'd sketched in. As she sat across from me, I flipped through the pages. "What'd you think?"

"Oh, they're *wonderful.*"

"What about this one?" I struggled to accept compliments, and when it came to critiques about my artwork, I was extra sensitive and prone to experiencing imposter syndrome.

She leaned over, fork in the air as she looked at the page I'd stopped on. One of the rough sketches for a simple sculpture.

"It's interesting. Makes me think of waves crashing."

Wow. That was precisely the sentiment I'd been hoping for. It represented the current stage of my life—being a hostage to lure my father to his death and wishing I didn't have to love a Mafia man who didn't desire me anymore.

"How does the process work? You draw it and then—" Margie stopped speaking as my phone rang. She looked up at me, furrowing her brow as I pulled the device closer.

Dammit. It was the same number Steven had used before. Ivan had suggested I label it so I wouldn't mistake the line of numbers as anything else. I'd almost laughed at him, ready to tell him *no one* else would be calling me. My former boss had probably dismissed me that night when I never showed up at the office again. Dominic likely deleted my number the second after he raped me. Then there was Steven.

"Ready?" the older woman asked. She was serious, pulling out her phone and ready to record the call on speaker. Just like before.

Ivan had instructed us both to record any other calls.

I nodded, hoping I *was* ready. Hearing Steven's voice was never a pleasant experience. He only called when he wanted something, and every time that happened, he was after something I wouldn't or couldn't give him.

"Hello." I didn't bother to infuse any enthusiasm into my greeting.

"Where the *fuck* are you?" he demanded.

I glanced at Emily, hoping she'd stay quiet and preoccupied with her food. She was, but her ever-watchful eyes were on my phone, probably alert with the man's harsh, mean tone.

"What do you want, Steven?" I didn't bother to reply to his question, tossing one out to him in kind.

"I want to know where you are, you stupid bitch."

Margie pressed her lips together, not liking the treatment he gave me.

"And I'm not revealing that information." *Thank God this device*

Dmitri is using blocks my location. I had no doubt he'd disabled it on my phone's settings, but I appreciated the second layer of security.

"Tell me where he is. Where is Ivan?"

I huffed, shaking my head. Holding up one hand to block Emily's view, I lifted my other hand and showed the phone the middle finger. Margie smirked, mildly amused as she rolled her eyes.

"I'm not telling you anything."

"You stupid whore! Tell me," he bellowed.

Emily dropped her baby spoon. Her lips pouted as she looked at me.

No. Don't cry. I didn't want a distraction while Steven called. This could be the break Ivan needed. If his call could be traceable, then he was a dead man. At the same time, I hated that I was subjecting Emily to hearing such vile nastiness.

Margie beat me to comforting my baby. She silently reached over to distract her by waving her spoon and making a silly face at her until she smiled.

You are an angel. I would never forget how good Margie was with Emily, how helpful she was at making me feel comfortable no matter what happened.

"Becca, you can't be this stupid. You have no idea what's at stake," he taunted.

I crossed my arms, staring at the call on speaker. "Then tell me. What *is* at stake, Steven?"

He snorted. "Stop being difficult."

I shook my head.

"Don't be such a gullible idiot and think you're better off siding with them."

Biting my lip, I watched Margie make Emily smile wider, pretending the spoon was a mute airplane.

"You're not," Steven said. "Do you even know what kind of a sicko Ivan Valkov is? Do you?"

He's a better man than you'll ever be.

"Do you know what you're doing by siding with those criminals?"

Ensuring my safety. The world will be a better place without you in it.

"He's a ruthless, violent man, Becca. He'll chew you up and spit you out like you're nothing."

I stayed silent.

"Because you *are* nothing!" His temper rose as his faint patience fell. "You hear me? You are *nothing* but a traitorous fucking bitch, a stupid whore to think you'd be better off siding with the Bratva. You are dead to me. Do you understand?"

No. I narrowed my eyes. *You are. And soon, you will literally be dead by Ivan's hands.*

"See if I give a shit," I retorted.

He growled.

"See if I give a damn about anything you say."

"I know what I'm talking about."

I fisted my hand. "I don't care! All you've ever wanted to do is use me."

"What the fuck do you think he's doing? Huh?" He raised his voice even louder. "He's only using you too."

To lure you out. And arguing with him, letting my emotions and anger get the better of me, wasn't helping.

"You're missing one difference there. He's not an abusive asshole like you."

"He's not?" Steven scoffed. "He's a sadistic freak who manages countless sex clubs in the city. He's a fucking meathead who tortures his enemies before he lets them die. And you want to be a dumb bitch and think he's some hero you can count on?"

"It's a lot better than ever counting on you."

He screamed, then hung up.

Once the call was done, Margie pressed the button on her phone to stop recording. "Oh, Becca..."

I covered my face, drawing in a steady breath. "I screwed that up."

"What? No." She took my free hand, and I looked up.

"Ivan told us to be prepared to record it, and we did. He said the longer we keep him on the phone, they might be able to trace the call."

I smirked. I knew that. But I'd lost my temper and prompted him

143

to hang up well before the length of time Dmitri had advised me to stay on for.

"I'm supposed to be bait," I told her. "Ivan is holding me hostage to make Steven come out of hiding."

She furrowed her brow, staring at me with sadness and rubbing the top of my hand.

"But it's not working. Steven doesn't care that I'm here. He just wants to know where Ivan is. I'm *not* serving any purpose as bait of any kind."

"No, that can't be true."

I sighed. "It is. Ivan captured me to hope that Steven would want to get me away from here. He clearly knows I'm with Ivan somewhere already, and it's not prompting him to reveal himself."

"It will all work out."

I swallowed hard, hating the idea that struck me. "But if I have no purpose here, Ivan will just… let me go."

"No." Margie shook her head firmly. "I don't see that happening. I can't begin to claim I know how these brothers work, how they oper-ate. They are always looking at the best angles to solving a problem, keeping on top of threats and potential issues. I am certain this… mission against Steven is more complicated than you or I can realize, but I do not think you are correct about Ivan dismissing you."

It'd become my biggest fear. Risking more honestly, I blinked back tears. "I don't want to. I don't want him to dismiss me anymore. I want him to see me, to want me to stay and…"

Emily knocked over her bowl from the high chair tray, and it jarred me from spilling my heart out to her. I already felt so raw from Steven's call. This confusion about what was happening didn't help. As I hurried to clean up the mess, Margie used a damp kitchen towel to wipe at her messy face, soothing her with soft words.

At the sink, she draped her arm around me and sighed.

"It will all work out as it should, Becca. I believe that."

I looked at her, hopeful yet skeptical. "You believe that Ivan would want to keep a woman like me?"

Her smile was slow but sure. "Yes."

From the bottom of my heart, I hoped so. I truly, earnestly wished that Ivan could show me mutual affection. If he stayed here long enough to just talk to me, to give me a chance to let him know that I was developing feelings for him, I'd lay my heart out to him and hope for the best.

"He would be a fool not to want you forever," Margie added.

"I'm so different." I shook my head. "Never mind the fact that my father is the enemy he wants to kill and my baby is the child of *another* of his enemies, I'm not like Ivan at all."

She crossed her arms. "How so?"

Embarrassment crept up my spine. "Well, he's at those sex clubs and used to, uh, stuff, and I'm pretty sheltered in that department."

"Bah." She dismissed me with a wave. "You can learn to compromise. He can teach you what he likes."

Oh, God. I felt so silly talking about this with her. She'd come to resemble a motherly figure, and it was strange chatting about sex with her.

"You're hardly the first person to be initiated into the Bratva. I was. Mila was. Amy was. Countless others have been brought into the Valkov Family for so many reasons. They are good men." She nodded, turning to the dishes in the sink. "They are lovable men, capable of loving the right women, too."

That's just it. How can I be the right woman for him?

"They fight hard. They work hard. And they love hard. From what I've seen, you are more than enough of a woman to make Ivan Valkov proud."

I smiled as I turned to Emily, praying this housekeeper angel was right.

And I looked forward to the first chance I might have to prove it to Ivan.

21

IVAN

Alek wanted another meeting about the potential issue of the drugs. Yusef came too, reporting a bunch of nothing. Murphy was not budging. He wasn't showing up anywhere.

"No one can care about him that much to hide him this well," Dmitri said.

I nodded. "It's making me wonder what he's working on."

"And if Becca is a part of it," Nik said.

I frowned at him and waited for him to clarify. "She's innocent in all of this."

He held his hand up. "I'm not implying she isn't. But it seems like we're missing something."

"I've felt like that ever since I took her."

"Let me get this straight." Maxim furrowed his brow. "Dom Rossini knocked her up and sent her home. No contact at all. And she has his kid."

"Yeah. Then what?" Alek prompted. "What's the connection? You think Rossini wants the baby?"

"Over my dead body," I growled.

They all looked at me. Nik grinned. Dmitri rolled his eyes. "Another one fallen for a magical pussy."

Nik, seated next to him, punched him hard.

"And it doesn't seem likely," I argued. "Why care about a bastard daughter now?"

"Besides the fact that Dom Rossini has knocked up countless women over the years," Alek added.

"Maybe that's why they're so prone to infighting and killing each other. They fuck like rabbits and repopulate," Dmitri joked.

"Have you talked to Becca again? To figure out if she knows anything else?" Nik asked.

I shook my head and sighed. "I've been trying to keep my distance." Sitting forward, I rubbed my face. "I can't stop thinking about her and wanting to—" I cut myself off, shaking my head. This wasn't the time for sappy shit.

"Then stop fighting it," Nik advised. "And talk to her. Even if she's a victim, even if she's not involved in anything, maybe she knows something without realizing its importance."

"If she spent months in Dom's company, even if he left her alone for most of it, she had to have noticed or heard something," Maxim said.

I stood, knowing they were right. I hated to talk about Dom or Steven with her again. Not only did it seem like we were just repeating the same thing over and over, my questions an echo to her non-changing and limited replies, I also wanted to avoid causing her to look so sad and hurt like she had when she told me that Dom raped her.

Back at the vacation home, I sought her out as soon as I closed the front door. "Becca?"

She was already coming toward me. It seemed she was eager to reach out to me directly too.

"What is it?" Her serious expression alarmed me.

"He called again." She lifted her old phone and the device connected to it. "But it still didn't trace. I'm sorry."

I nodded, taking it and also grabbing her hand. The contact of her smaller fingers alongside mine teased me, but I resisted the urge to hold her closer. This call had to come first, and I wanted her to stay with me as I listened to it. "Where's Emily?" I asked as I led Becca to my room.

"With Margie. Finger paints in the kitchen."

Good. I didn't want any interruptions.

In my room, I gestured for her to sit in a chair near the fireplace that waited empty and cold for the far-off winter months. I paced, playing the recording she'd sent to herself from Margie's phone. It wasn't the most high-tech solution, but it worked. I wanted to avoid bringing too many men out here to improve it. I already worried that my coming and going here would be a weakness for Murphy or anyone else to notice. I didn't need more men in and out of here for anyone to try to break in or even know that we were here.

Walking back and forth through my room, I listened to the call. Over and over. I replayed it, filing all of Steven's angry words to memory.

Becca sat stiffly, frowning at the empty fireplace until I felt confident I would remember it all.

"He's such a despicable bastard," she muttered.

"You're not stupid."

She rolled her eyes. "I don't care what he said about me. I know I'm not dumb. He's called me names and tried to belittle me my whole life."

I tilted my head to the side, loving this stubborn defense she had for herself. Seeing a woman recognize and stand by her self-worth was admirable and sexy as hell.

"What about what he said of me?"

She looked me up and down, a once-over from my shoes to the top of my head. "He doesn't know you." After clearing her throat, she sighed. "He doesn't know you like I do. Even though I want to learn more."

Fuck me. The longing in her voice cut through me. I wanted to show her all of me. Everything. I wanted to strip bare and welcome her into my life for good.

I went to her, lowering to one knee, and took her hand. Her paler, softer skin cut such a contrast to my darker flesh marred with ink and scars. "And you *can* count on me."

She had to know this by now. I'd told her that her purpose was to be a hostage, bait, but she'd come to be so much more.

"I've noticed..." She almost smiled, but the topic of her father had her frowning again.

I squeezed her hand before standing, pacing once more to think better.

"He's just trying to get a rise out of you."

"I suspected that." She slumped back in her seat. "And that's not the first time he's tried to get me to lower my guard by hurling insults and demands."

"It's almost like he's trying to distract you," I added.

"But why? For what reason? Distract me from what?" She cringed. "I don't see what I can have to do with his need to hide like this."

"Think back. Let's talk it all out."

She growled. "I've already told you everything I know."

"Be patient." I glanced at her as I took the other chair, leaning forward to set my elbows on my knees and my hands held together. "Start with the clubs."

She smirked. "I don't go to clubs."

"But he wanted you to get an envelope for him at one."

"Yeah, but I hung up on him. I don't know what that would've been for, who would've given me anything, nor which club he'd expected me to go to."

I nodded. "What about your time with Dom? You didn't hear him mention Murphy during all that time?"

She shook her head. "Just that one time. That night he... he raped me. And I didn't hear him mention Steven's name. I just overheard them talking and I recognized Steven's voice on the speaker call."

"Dom never asked you anything about him?"

"Never. Nothing."

I wouldn't give up. "What did he talk about?"

"Not much. I spent more time speaking with assistants at galleries and meeting instructors and students at universities. Dom was a busy businessman, just arranging my lodging as he traveled around. We'd have dinners and such, enough for him to try to charm me into spending more time with him."

What aren't you saying, though? "You said that he admitted to only being interested in you as a way to keep an eye on Murphy."

She nodded, furrowing her brow. "Yes."

"But if he never asked you about Murphy, how was he keeping tabs on him?"

She shrugged, lifting her phone. "I don't know. Maybe hoping Steven would contact me and they could trace my calls? I don't know. When I came home, before I found out I was pregnant, I wondered if Dominic might have intended to keep me with him as insurance. If he and Steven were working on something together but argued and didn't see eye to eye on details, maybe Dominic wanted to keep me close as a way to keep Steven in line."

Which sounds a lot like what I figured to do as well, to use her to lure him out of hiding.

"But they sounded like they'd ended whatever plan they had."

"Okay. Then what *did* Dominic talk about with you?" *There's got to be something useful from her time with that fucker.*

Her shoulders lifted and fell. "Art."

"You talked about art?"

How the fuck would that ever matter? Still, I had to keep trying and keep pushing. I refused to admit defeat.

"Yeah. Pretty much."

I sighed. "Then tell me about it. Tell me about your art and whatever you remember discussing with him."

22

BECCA

"What *we* discussed?" I rolled my eyes. "We never discussed anything in a back-and-forth manner." I flicked my finger between us. "It wasn't a give-and-take conversation. Nine times out of ten, he'd lecture. And provide a lengthy explanation of his opinions. Why *he* thought one style was too old and unrelatable to care about and how *he* planned to acquire a variety of artists to sponsor all through Europe."

Ivan smirked. "He does seem like the sort of man who enjoys hearing himself talk."

I nodded. "Wait. Have you ever met him? Dom?"

"No. Not in person. I've, uh, dealt with plenty of other men and leaders within their organization, but Dominic travels too much. He's hardly ever in the States."

"That sounds about right. He was always on the go, and I was so curious what the hell he did to be so rich but never actually work."

Because he was a Mafia Don. A member of the goddamn Italian Mob.

"He patronized me. I was so swept away by the grandeur of having someone 'in my corner' and seeing Europe that I was sucked in for too long."

"Did he ever look at your art?" he asked.

I nodded. "Not much. I showed him what I had made, what I wanted to do." A laugh bubbled inside me. "But he never once came to my studio. At first, I was embarrassed to bring him there. It's such a small little dump. But any sponsor worth his word would've wanted to see where I made my artwork." Shaking my head, I loathed the sting of the entire experience. Hindsight was a bitch like that. Looking back, I saw so many red flags that I should've paid attention to.

"Your studio?"

"Yeah."

"I didn't know you had a studio." He furrowed his brow.

I smiled slightly. "Well, you don't know *me* that well."

His gaze turned hot as he looked me over. His stare was like a physical, sensual caress. Just like that, I was aroused, wanting his touch on me again.

"I followed you. To know how to best take you and keep you from Murphy's reach."

The way he said that seemed odd. "From Steven's reach?" He said it like Steven was trying to do something to me or expecting something from me.

"Yeah." He cleared his throat and stood.

I couldn't be sure because he turned, but I thought I saw a bulge of his erection beneath his pants.

"Where's this studio?"

"It was my grandmother's. It's never been in my name, and Steven never cared about it." I stood as well, curious where he was going. Was he running off because he let an inkling of desire come to mind? Was he that repulsed by me?

"Can we go there?"

I blinked. "What? Why?"

"So I can see your artwork."

I followed him toward the door. Having an opportunity to spend time with him alone sounded like the dream I wanted to come true. "But why?"

"That's the connection you had to Dom. And if Murphy is working with Dom or targeting him specifically, then that's a direct way for me to get to him." He paused at the door, stopping so suddenly that I slammed into him.

I craned my neck to look up at him, peering into his dark gaze.

"And the faster I remove him…"

I swallowed. "Then you can be rid of me? And Emily?" I had no right to pose that question to him, but I wanted to know. I had to know.

He tipped his head to the side, staring at me with such intensity.

"Is that what you want?" he asked, licking his lips as he locked his heated gaze on mine.

Breathing was difficult. My heart raced so fast. His direct attention unnerved me in the best of ways, but I felt overwhelmed, torn between answering honestly but not sounding too desperate and clingy.

"I want…" God, I couldn't say it. I'd never been able to make a request or ask for anything for myself. Doing so felt dangerous, like he'd use the knowledge of my desire for him against me.

He sighed, taking my hand as he turned and left the room with me. "Margie can stay with Emily. Where is this studio?"

I told him, wincing when he shot me an incredulous look. "I know. It's not a great area of the city."

"Deep in the Cartel's territory," he commented with a hard look.

"It was my grandmother's studio."

After we checked with Margie that she'd gladly stay with Emily and watch her, I left with Ivan. It was strange to leave the house, and he noticed, still holding my hand.

"I'm not going to run," I said as he led me to the car in the garage.

He held on tighter anyway. "I know."

So… you enjoy holding my hand? For the hell of it? I fought a smile, too giddy with this one-eighty of attention.

Once we were in the car, I felt the heat of his gaze on me as I buckled.

"What?" I brushed my hair back as I looked up at him, unsure how to navigate this moment. He looked at me with such desire, but a guardedness he wouldn't give up on.

"Nothing." He drove, and after a few awkward minutes of quiet, he turned to me. "How did your grandmother get this studio?"

I settled into the seat, glad to talk about someone in my family I wasn't ashamed of. "Her grandparents bought it for her. My mother's side of the family is a long one of hardships. Coming to the US as immigrants, toughing out new beginnings and all. I believe the basement space was important for the prohibition times. My great-great grandfather was an officer, and he kept the area that his wife turned into a pottery space. The kiln had been updated, but the purpose of the room remained the same."

"You come from a long line of cops?" he asked.

"Yes and no. Many of them served in law enforcement, but just as many didn't. My grandfather was actually Steven's boss." My chipper mood fell. "They never got along, and no wonder. Steven is as crooked as they come. I still think he set up my mother to die."

"How did she die?"

"In a car accident. It was right after my grandfather punished Steven on the force, and it seemed too convenient of a timing. Like payback. A week later, my grandfather passed away, probably the strain of grief of losing his only child. Then my grandmother had a stroke and could no longer get around well enough to see to my care. I was stuck with Steven, and that was that."

He took my hand and squeezed it again. "I'm sorry."

I sighed, loving his tender touch. "It is what it is."

"I lost my mother too soon. And my father was killed by another family member."

I shook my head. "I guess we're not too different, after all."

He released my hand. "Yeah, right."

My heart sank at his faint laughter. Like it was crazy talk to make myself relatable to him.

"You're light and I'm dark. You're innocent and naïve, and I've lived a life of too many ugly experiences I'll never forget."

I tucked my hands together between my thighs, wishing I could cower away from his stark descriptions. I was an idiot to ever think we would mesh.

"That's why I've tried to stay away, Becca." He blew out a long and loud sigh, venting as he drove. "After I brought you here, I knew I'd get addicted to teaching you, showing you what I liked."

I shrugged, looking out the window.

"Because I fucking loved every second of pounding into your tight pussy. Every minute of feeling you surrender to me."

I squeezed my legs tighter together, turned on by his filthy talk.

"But I knew you weren't mine. You're supposed to be a hostage, not the first and only woman who'd get under my skin."

I whipped around to stare at him, mesmerized by his gritty honesty that he seemed so annoyed about.

"That you'd never be mine. Too good and sweet. Too different from the hard life I'm used to."

"Then make me tougher. Dirty me up."

He faced me, capturing me with his hooded gaze. I reveled in his needy expression, like he'd been tormenting himself to stay away.

"Don't tempt me." He returned his focus to the road.

Too late. I squirmed in my seat. *Because you've tempted me since the moment you first tied me up.*

We didn't speak for the rest of the drive, and I vacillated between wanting to speak up and staying quiet. He'd given me so much to think about, but I was too nervous to get my hopes up high. This was complicated, being near him and realizing we might have mutual desire for each other. Steven was the biggest obstacle, but once he was gone and Ivan no longer had a reason to keep me so close…

One thing at a time. I'd take this conversation as a positive thing, a step in the right direction for what my heart and body wanted.

He drove straight to the studio, and my excitement about being here increased.

"I let a college student come in when she needs to work on things. Someone Hannah knows. But she broke her wrist recently, and I doubt she's been in here." Unlocking the door to the basement space was a familiar routine that I hadn't done in a while.

"Have you been here recently?" he asked as he followed me in and blinked at the bright lights flickering on as I hit the switch.

It smelled stale, unused, but the further we entered, the fragrant scent of earthy, muddy clay hit me and I smiled.

"No. Not since Emily was born. I came here maybe once when I was pregnant." I hated that I'd been gone for so long. How could I ever become a full-time artist if I was never present to make new things?

"It's not easy, working sixty hours a week and then being a single parent." I glanced at him as he walked around, looking at the paintings, drawings, and unfinished sculpture designs. "I never had a Margie to help."

Or you.

"Do you paint and sculpt and draw?" He claimed a stool and sat on it, watching me flit around the creative space I'd missed.

"All of the above. I paint, but I prefer sculpture. Working with my hands." I grabbed a piece of clay from the airtight bin, assuming he wouldn't mind if I demonstrated what I meant.

Seated at the wheel, I wetted the plate to begin securing the clay for a simple bowl.

"How come?"

I shrugged without lifting my hands. "I like to *feel* it. To feel the art come alive."

He stared, watching my hands with obvious curiosity. "I know what you mean."

I arched a brow. "Oh, you spend time molding clay too?" I teased. He was far too serious of a man to seem like an artist. He didn't even seem like a person who'd lighten up enough to have a hobby of any kind.

"No. People." He lifted his gaze to me, and I almost shivered under the smolder in his dark eyes. "I like to feel a woman come alive under my hands, restrained by my bindings."

Oh, hell. I swallowed, my mouth dry at his naughty talk.

"I like to shape and mold the shyest and most stubborn woman to come alive and welcome a little brutality to really soar."

I licked my lips, too intimidated to face him and hear such wanton desires. If he wasn't talking about me, then I'd have to curl my lip with anger and jealousy. But if he was taunting me, I wasn't sure I could withstand the teasing.

"But we're not talking about me." He sighed, crossing his arms. "We were talking about art. Your sculptures. Paintings."

I smiled, amused by his abrupt attempt to focus on something else. Like he couldn't take the heat as well.

But why resist it? Why not just give in? I wanted to, so badly. But I was too shy to be that open and admit that I wanted him to encourage me to come alive under his rough touch.

"This is what you enjoy?" he asked, almost sarcastic.

I nodded, glancing up at him. "Yeah. I do."

"Making something out of a blob."

I hated the teasing tone he said that with. I'd been so eager, wishing he'd be genuinely interested about something I held dear, about something that would show him who I was. My passion. My calling.

But I had to check myself and remember he had made a point in the car. We *were* different. He dealt with life-or-death situations and decided on heavier, graver choices than this. He never eased up to be the kind of person to debate about which tools to use or how to style something to be thought-provoking and aesthetic.

That was what art was about.

That was what inspired me to improve.

But he doesn't care. He can't.

Just like Dom. Ivan didn't care about my artwork and what it meant to me.

He'd only come here mildly intrigued, looking for a clue or connection about my past that somehow mattered to his future of killing Steven.

"You'd never be mine."

He'd stated that with deep conviction on the ride here, and I felt like a fool a thousand times over not to understand it, to resist it and wish otherwise.

23

IVAN

I couldn't look away.

Becca sat there comfortable and confident, at ease with a natural-born grace. She belonged there, in her element and relaxed behind that spinning wheel.

And I refused to miss a second of it.

It was a huge step to approach after trying to distance myself while she was in my custody. Staying busy and away from her hadn't helped this obsession with her. It had only fueled my desire.

Giving in and seeking her out was a big change in my treatment toward her. Alek expected me to talk to her again and try to ferret out more information about Steven. But I was here with a different perspective.

I was a moron to ever try to stay away from her in the hopes that my intrigue and lust for her would fade.

And all those weeks were nothing but wasted time I could have spent talking with her, fucking her, falling even further.

No wonder Alek and Nik were unashamed to show how much Mila and Amy mattered to them.

This feeling of clicking with a woman was soul deep. I'd never felt so aware and certain with another person, and I would be damned if I'd let anything prevent me from getting closer to her.

We were different. But maybe she could be the yin to my yang and complete me like no other.

"How did you learn to do that?" I asked, my focus rapt on her.

Her slender fingers were strong and confident over the clay. Those toned arms showed her musculature, all the smaller, finer motions she'd honed with finesse in her line of work. With her red hair falling out of that bun, cascading down to almost shelter her sweet face from my view, she looked like a fairy. A siren. An earthy, sexy woman of art and compassion.

An innocent lover who welcomed me to make her harder. To dirty her up.

I'd fucking love to, Becca. You have no idea how much I want to.

"I watched videos. Hung out at the art room at school." She made it sound like it was nothing, like just anyone could merely witness someone else performing this craft and instantly pick up on it themselves.

"Steven was never there. I was a latch-key kid, left to my own devices, expected to raise myself and take care of anything I needed. He never knew or cared where I was. Never knew that I'd taken an interest in art.

"Did your grandmother teach you too?" I asked, wishing I could take the chance to get closer to her. She called to me, enticing me to touch her. It wasn't easy to watch her capable hands slippery on that dark clay and not wish that she could touch me the same. Hard, with a firm grip. Rubbing and stroking. Unafraid to use pressure and create what she wanted. It would be like a kneading massage. Or an irresistible tug on my cock. All I could think of as I watched her fingers was the vision of her gripping me, of her cupping her own tits and squeezing herself to the point of pain.

Art was a delicate study. A dainty pastime. Seeing her at it, though, I wanted to watch her go further and use more force. To take her own sexuality with both hands, unafraid to explore like she did with this clay.

"She did. But that was so long ago. When my mother was alive, she spent so much of her time with me. Going to bookstores. The park. The library. Anywhere free and away from Steven because he'd never treated her well, always arguing and fighting."

"She tried to shelter you from him?" I guessed.

"Yes. And she'd bring me to visit my grandma here and there. But my grandma disliked Steven and always thought he'd conned my mother into dating and marrying her. She claimed that he'd knocked her up for control."

I wondered if she'd ever thought that about Dominic and Emily. But that didn't ring true. The man hadn't even known she had his daughter. He'd dismissed her.

"After my mother was gone, I was too ruled with grief to spend time on art. My grandmother had her stroke, and that prevented her from showing me much. It's a blessing she left me this place, though, for the little I ever use it."

I could see her here, and in a better location. Somewhere with windows. More security. Not in the basement of an old building on the Cartel's turf.

That was an addicting dream to latch on to. Giving her the world. Making her happy.

"If you could have the freedom to focus on your art, is that what you'd like to do?"

She glanced up at me, doubt and skepticism in her green eyes. "It's not *all* I'd want to do."

"What else?"

She sighed, lowering her gaze again. The curtained effect of her hair lent her an air of mystery, of luring me to see her sweet eyes again, so open and vulnerable. She was too soft, too delicate, and a burning need to protect her and show her the world lit hotter within me.

"I hated being an only child. I'd love to have a family for once. For Emily to not only depend on me, but several others who'd love her just the same."

I laughed once. "Trust me. As one of five boys, sometimes, having siblings isn't all it's cracked up to be."

She smiled. Her cheeks lifted slightly as she kept her focus on the clay blob that already resembled the shape of a bowl.

"You want to have more children?" I asked.

She huffed a laugh. "Well, isn't this getting to be a deep and introspective interview?"

It was. And I was enjoying every second of it. I'd spent too many years maintaining walls around my heart. To kill, torture, and hunt like I was expected to, I had to harden my heart and protect my soul. With her, this woman almost thirteen years younger than me, I felt safe to be honest for the first time ever.

"I never thought I'd have kids."

She raised her brows. "Do you?"

I shook my head.

She seemed flustered, licking her lips and lowering her head. "You, uh, you didn't use a condom with me."

"I didn't."

She glanced up at my statement. "On... purpose?"

"No. It just happened. But I would've given you a contraceptive pill afterward if I'd wanted to."

"You mean to tell me that a man who supervises sex clubs, someone with a much more varied sex life than the norm, who surely sleeps around a lot, has never knocked anyone up?"

I shook my head. "I use protection. And if I don't, I demand the morning-after contraception. No exceptions."

Her hands didn't move, still over the spiraling bowl. "Other than me?"

"Other than you." Part of my decision had been an impulse of figuring nothing would happen. When I fucked her for the purpose of getting her to talk, I figured it'd be the only time I'd have her or even want her.

How wrong I was.

Since that night, I'd yearned for another time with her. And another. And more.

When I did consider forcing her to take a contraceptive pill the morning after, I dismissed the thought. Too many things were happening. I learned that she was already a mother, and the process of her getting under my skin was already too far underway for me to not want a future with her.

"Seeing you with Emily has changed me," I admitted.

"How so?" Her question came quickly, but softly.

"She's innocent, so trusting, and I feel like a fucking king when I calm her down or see her smile."

"It is marvelous, isn't it? Not only the satisfaction of knowing you helped her and the reward of stopping her from fussing, but it also feels so good to be the one to provide and fix things."

I nodded. That was it. I knew just what she meant.

"I hate the thought of your having to do it all alone." I grunted a laugh. "Obviously. That's why I called Margie and asked her to come to the house to help."

"She's an angel."

But am I your hero?

"I can't imagine being a single parent."

"Because of what you have to do for your family? For your job?"

"Not only that. But because I'd want to share the experience. With a partner."

I watched her slender neck tense as she swallowed. Once more, she broke eye contact, and it felt like a crime to hide away from me.

I'd started on this path, and I refused to stop.

"I've been thinking about how I don't want to see her go. That I want to be able to watch her grow up and develop into a young girl, then a headstrong woman."

She sighed, furrowing her brow as she focused on the bowl.

"How I want to see you open up to me. To trust me to show how good it can be past the pain."

"Ivan..."

I stood, unable to sit here with this tense attraction hanging between us. We'd both resisted this for too damn long. This suspense of not being together was too damn much to bear anymore.

"I keep wondering what you might think if you ignored how different we are." I walked closer, heady with the tease of being within her reach.

"I torment myself with wanting to ask you to stay."

She lifted her face to me as I stood before her, next to the still-spinning wheel. The lust shining in her eyes was the final straw. Even if she'd try to insist she didn't want me, I saw it. I felt this snapping electricity between us.

"After Murphy is gone. Once I kill Dominic—"

Her jaw dropped. "Dom? Him too?"

I nodded. "For ever fucking touching you." Lowering my hand, I cupped her chin and slid my hand over the soft slope of her jaw. Such a heart-shaped, perfectly angelic face. This woman would be the death of me, dammit. I craved her with every cell of my body.

"You'd do that?" She swallowed, tipping her face up higher to stare at me. "For... me?"

"For you and Emily. For my peace of mind to know that no other man can ever claim you again."

She tugged her lower lip between her teeth, and I reached up with my thumb to free the plump flesh. I'd be the one to bite her, dammit.

"How can I know that you mean it?" She blinked, wary but seeming so tired of fighting what she wanted. "How can I know that you really want me, Ivan?"

I gripped her, holding on to the underside of her jaw to prompt her to rise.

"I'll fucking you show you, sweetheart."

Then I crashed my lips to hers and sucked down her needy growl in response.

24

BECCA

I struggled to stand, tugged upward with Ivan's big, strong hand under my chin. He didn't choke me, but the pressure was unforgiving. While he didn't need to try so hard to prompt me to meet him in the middle, I relished the hint of his dominance.

I wanted him to lead me. I longed for him to take me how he wanted because I knew how good it would feel in the end.

We crashed, our mouths smashing against each other. And my heart sang. My pussy clenched and dripped. In a split second, I was aroused and rabid for him.

After hearing him explain that he saw something more than a hostage situation in store for me, I fought with the excitement of my dreams coming true.

Of knowing he wanted me.

Lusted for me.

And truly hoped to keep me in his life. Not just me, but Emily too. Ivan wanted us for good, as a package deal, and I was all for this vision of a happier life with him.

"You want to know how you can believe me?" he growled, stepping back to breathe heavily as he stared down at me.

I nodded, unable to move my head much with his fingers wrapped around my throat. "Please," I begged.

He grunted, wrapping his arms around me as he walked forward. I stumbled, clinging to him and arching up into his kiss. Into the incessant pressure of his hot, hungry lips devouring mine.

The backs of my thighs smacked into the edge of the work table, and I let out a deep breath at the impact. Pinned between his hard body and the rough-cut edge of the surface, I felt stuck and immobile. That didn't stop me from reaching up and twining my arms around his neck. It didn't prevent me from moaning into his mouth and accepting the hiss of pain when he nipped my bottom lip.

"I'll show you," he promised.

Without giving me a chance to reply, he gripped my hips and hoisted me up onto the table. Tools shook in the cups off to the side. Dust puffed up from previous projects I'd completed on the other corner of the plywood-constructed surface.

My ass stung with the hard drop onto the bare wood, but I didn't linger on the sensation for long. I couldn't. Not when he tugged my dress collar so hard that buttons went flying, that the fabric ripped near the seams. The material hung to the sides like a cloak, and I parted my legs as he stepped closer.

Breathing hard and panting quickly, he stared at me with unbridled lust shining in his eyes. He dragged his hands from my shoulders down my arms, pushing my garment off more. Then he cupped my breasts, lowering to suck hard on my nipples one at a time until I knew I'd be streaking a trail of fluids on the surface of the table.

He wasn't finished, shoving his hands lower over my stomach until he bunched my panties in his fists. One forceful tug ripped them, and I parted my legs easily for him to look at my pussy.

A wicked, carnal grin changed his face. He eyed me, taking in the wet entrance that beckoned him, and I shivered in anticipation.

"You want to know how you can trust that I want you?"

I exhaled a quick, breathy whoosh of air as he trailed his fingers up and down my slit, teasing me. "Yes, Ivan. Show me how much you want me, please."

"Not just like this," he growled, pushing me to scoot back on the table. "But *always*."

I leaned back, shaky with need. Desire controlled me, and I couldn't wait for him to take over that power and commandeer it as he saw fit. Whatever he wanted, I knew it would be good for me.

"Hold on to the other side of the table."

I reached up, scraping my nails to claw for the edge. His hand lay heavy on my stomach, pushing down so I'd be flat. Once I found the table's edge, I held on tight.

He lowered immediately, replacing his fingers with his tongue, his lips, then his teeth, too. He sucked and licked with precision, laving my tender flesh with a hunger I wished he'd always have for me.

Tension built and burned as my pussy throbbed and ached. My pulse was already so fast, and I feared my heart couldn't keep up with the intense suspense and buildup to what would likely be a brutal orgasm.

"You see?" he taunted, looking up at me with my juices glistening on his chin. "You see how fucking hungry I am for you?"

I groaned, arching into his hand as he thrust his fingers in. It felt too good. So damned wonderful and thrilling, yet not enough.

"I see."

He leaned over. I registered the press of his side on my leg, and I wondered if he was done eating me out. I wasn't there yet. I needed more. I wanted to come so damn badly after all these weeks of pining for him.

"And do you feel?" he asked in a gravelly tone as he slipped something hard into my cunt.

I tensed, breathing faster as I tried to understand what he was doing. Opening my eyes slowly, I took in the wicked sight of him sliding a sculpting tool into me. The smooth, polished handle was easily the size of three of his fingers. At the top, sticking outside me and resting in his hand, was the circular metal loop that sliced into clay.

Oh, God.

The handle fit into me just as well as his fingers did. Hard and thick. Deep and steady.

"Oh… fuck." I was incapable of any further speech. He was so dirty, so impulsive, and not afraid to give it to me hard.

He held the open sharp loop, plunging the tool's handle up into me at the same time he circled my clit with his fingers, rubbing so perfectly, so quickly, that I came in no time.

"You feel how I can make you fly?"

Keening cries of pleasure were all I could manage. Speech was impossible. Thoughts ceased to fill my mind. I writhed and bucked, quivering with the intensity of coming after such a long dry spell.

"And I will never stop," he promised, shedding his pants. The zipper was so loud. The drag over the surface, rough and unsanded, burned under my ass.

"Never," I agreed, reaching for him limply as wave after wave of bliss crashed through me. I couldn't catch my breath, suspended in this weightless feeling of floating and sinking at the same time.

He dragged me further to the edge of the table, lifting my legs into the air as he lined up the tip of his dick.

"I will fuck the doubt out of you, sweetheart."

Then he proceeded to do just that. With one hard drive in, he sank his cock into me. I groaned, tensing at the full, hard hit of his length so deep inside me. Just like before, he didn't give me a chance to adjust, to acclimate to this hard, delicious stretch.

In and out, he pounded into me. Gripping my legs, he dug his fingers into my flesh. His nails pressed into my skin. Sweat slicked between my ass and the rough board. My hair tugged and pinched as it caught on the grain of the wood. All the while, I clung to the other edge of the table, holding on for dear life as my muscles quivered from the strain.

"You hear me?" he rasped, squeezing my legs more as he sped up his full, brutal thrusts into me.

He showed no mercy. He gave me no pause. Straight into me. Over and over again.

"You're going to fucking come for me, good girl. You're going to squeeze my dick with that tight pussy and milk me."

"Yes. Yes." I panted, my need to come apart so blindingly bright that I thought I'd pass out.

"I'm gonna flood your cunt with my cum and you're going to take it all."

I cried out, overwhelmed with his filthy talk and the abrasive pushes on the wood. His penis impaled me, sheathing inside my slick walls, and I couldn't hold on much longer. He was too thick, too fast, pushing into me and upward in just the right way that I splintered into a thousand pieces of bliss.

"Ivan!" Wetness dripped down my cheeks. Tears of joy couldn't be held back as he thrust in twice more and came right after me. My orgasm wasn't short. With waves of pleasure as our combined juices squelched out of me, I went lax and let the sensations course through me. The fullness of him embedded so deep. The tug of his fingers on my legs as he kept me close. The friction of his hairy thighs as my ass rested against him.

I couldn't move because he still held on to me. And I didn't want to, either. He'd fucked me so hard and fast, I could only try to breathe and recover from the intensity, from the suspense of wanting to explode on him.

He slipped out once he staggered to lie over me. His head rested on my chest, rising and falling with my quick breath. Together, we rested and came down from the high of a quick, much-overdue fuck. Without words, skipping anything sweet and tender, we simply stuck there together, sated and depleted of energy after snapping that tension simmering between us.

He'd wanted to show me that I could trust that he wanted me for good. Even though that was just sex, physical, I felt the determination in every moment of his touch.

I ran my hand over his head, stroking his hair back, and sighed.

Finally, he stood, wincing at the awkward slump over the table. Still without speaking, he offered me a hand to help me sit up, then to stand.

As he checked my back and legs for scrapes and splinters from the wood, I held on to him and felt our cum slipping out of my pussy. It dribbled on the insides of my thighs, and I staggered toward the sink for some paper towels.

I couldn't believe I caved. And I was stunned that I still wanted more. It seemed I would never get enough of him, and I tried to let that idea fade away. He said he wanted me, and I had no reason not to believe him. He may never be a man of many words, but he sure as hell proved his feelings through his forceful actions.

"Dom was never here?" he asked after we cleaned up near the sink.

He'd pulled his pants on, and I paused in the process of buttoning the remaining closures on my dress.

"What?" My heart iced over.

"Dom." He glanced at me. "Was Dom ever in here?"

I'd already told him that he never came here. Was he implying that I fucked men in this studio all the time? Ivan was the only man I'd ever let in here. This was my private, personal space that mattered to me, and it had felt so special sharing it with him, letting him see me for who I really was as I dared to take that chance of opening up to him.

"What the hell?"

All the warm glow of having sex with him and believing his words about wanting me for good faded. My mood vanished. A cold anger replaced it.

"I told you he wasn't here. Dom wasn't in my life like that."

I'd never wanted to sleep with him, and I hated that Ivan could be insinuating that I had. His question made me bristle. He'd asked because that was all he needed from me. All he wanted from me—information about his enemies.

I was a moron to fall for his sweet words and think that he was telling the truth when he said he saw a future with me and Emily.

I will never fucking learn. A man could promise me the world and I'd be a sucker, so desperate for a better life.

All Ivan wanted was intel, and he could be bothered to slow down for a quick fuck along the way to getting it.

"Let me get this straight. You fucked me to loosen me up so I'd give you information you still think I'm withholding from you."

He scowled. "No. That's not it at all."

"The hell it isn't."

"Fuck this bullshit, Becca. I didn't. All I care about doing is figuring out what I'm missing before you or anyone else gets hurt."

I stared at him as he smoothed down his shirt, wishing I could know whether he was telling the truth. I believed him when he said he wanted me. I felt the evidence of his arousal and how determined he was to make me come.

Then why did he have to jump right back to asking me about Dom? I didn't understand, and for the drive back to the vacation villa, I lingered in a twisted sense of dread and confusion.

25

IVAN

Two days later, after I'd thought I'd reached an important step of explaining to Becca that she was holding *me* hostage by capturing my heart, I sighed heavily and slumped in the chair at the table at the family's mansion.

She'd gotten so damn mad, and it had taken me a full night of restless sleep to think back and understand why.

Becca was always on my mind, deep in my heart, and it had hurt when she'd blown up at me after I'd fucked her on that table. I'd taken her the way I had to show her with my desire how badly I coveted her, and she'd taken it the wrong way in the end.

After we came, and when I'd asked her again if Dom had ever been in that studio, I'd inquired because I was jealous. I wanted to think that I was the only man to really ever *see* Becca, to be invited into her special place and share intimacy there.

Knowing she wanted me in that place felt like a reward, and I wanted to get used to the idea of being the *only* man to ever go there.

But I saw how she likely assumed I was just after information for the sake of wars and vendettas, for the purpose of being a step ahead of my enemies.

Asking about Dom so soon after we'd had that deep conversation, after we'd told each other what we saw for ourselves in the future, she would've wondered about my intentions.

Because we started our relationship unconventionally, with her as my hostage in the matter of business, we would always have that past to overcome, that lingering lack of trust in the beginning.

I couldn't blame her for being so on edge and suspicious. Especially after the lifelong treatment Murphy gave her—asking her to do favors, then Dom manipulating her where her heart lay.

She would need time to get used to the fact that my feelings for her were sincere, that I wanted her for a selfish reason unlike what her father and her rapist had in mind.

I wanted Becca because she completed me. Because with her, knowing I might have her love in return, I was a better and stronger man.

No time for it now.

Right now, I had to push back the headache of making up with her and expressing myself clearer. I was here for a discussion about business, and it wasn't looking good.

I'd been busy with more issues at the clubs, and now I had to take a meeting with Alek about the increase of drugging incidents.

I was the last to arrive, coming straight from LeVant's and checking with Kenneth that he would be extra cautious tonight. Even though it seemed like they'd been waiting for me, I stayed quiet while the rest of the brothers greeted me.

"We've got to stay on top of this," Alek began.

I nodded. That was what I was doing yesterday and today, dealing with the news of a few more people being drugged at clubs, including one of ours. Two men had died so far, and one woman might not make it. "I'm trying."

Once this got to the news, we'd be facing lots of trouble. From law enforcement. The Feds. Even our clientele. The news of bad drugs at our clubs would scare off our guests from being members and visiting. Money made the world go round, and we had to be wise about how to deflect this rising potential of bad press.

Alek was furious, drumming his fingers on the table.

I was livid too. This was personal now, my avenue of the Bratva organization under fire. This was no longer a simple hiccup we could overcome.

Dmitri summed it up perfectly. "Someone's setting up the Bratva to take the fall for this."

"And it's got to stop." Alek leaned forward in his seat, eyeing me for a long moment. "*Now.*"

Goddammit. I know that.

"Drugs had never been an issue," Nik said. "But this hardcore shit sounds like it's going to be a problem that we can't wait out to finish on its own."

Obviously. We wouldn't stop the drug trade completely, but we had to figure out who was dropping this nasty shit near or at our clubs. The Bratva was in this to make money, like any other corporation, but we only planned to do so with the typical drugs that were already available elsewhere. Not this experimental crap that seemed to be a lab product.

It was killing customers. And Alek was right. It had to stop now. Not tomorrow. Not after we found Murphy and I killed him. We had to end this before further damage brought us down.

"What if someone goes undercover at a club?" Maxim suggested. He glanced at me, facing me directly. "Maybe it's doing more harm than good for you to show up. So many people on the club scene know you and recognize you. These drugs might not pass hands when you're around for that reason."

I nodded, sighing. "I was thinking that too." I was viewed as the Bratva's representative at all the clubs.

"Undercover?" Nik winced, rubbing his jaw. "I don't think I can. Not right now."

He was our stealthy man. Wearing disguises was his specialty.

He shook his head, glancing at Alek. "Amy's struggling again with the pregnancy, and the doctor thinks it's best if I stay by her and keep her blood pressure as low as possible this close to her due date."

"I wouldn't ask you," Alek said quickly. He understood the tension of caring for a pregnant wife. Mila was going to deliver any day now.

I raised my hand, waving at them to remind them that I was right here. "No. I've got it." The sex clubs had always been my responsibility. I hated to think these drugs were getting in because I was distracted by Becca. Falling in love was a new experience for me, but I had to do better with compartmentalizing. I wouldn't fail my family now.

"But that's what we're saying," Nik said. "It can't be you."

I smirked at him. "I know that. I can't be identified. But I can use a disguise too."

They nodded in agreement.

"Or instead of stopping in at one of our regular clubs," I added, "I could try to go to that place we just sold. The club we sold uptown. Veronica told me she thinks she was drugged there. No one would expect to see me there, and people might not be on guard as much."

Alek seemed to like that idea. "When you first mentioned a drugging happening there, I wondered if someone was trying to frame us even then. Because that club *had* been ours until very recently."

I'd wondered that too. "If you consider the facts, it's somewhere these fuckers already peddled the drugs. So I want to assume the odds are high that they might try again since they successfully did it once," I explained.

"You sure you want to handle it?" Dmitri asked.

I furrowed my brow. "Why wouldn't I?"

He shrugged. "Just with Becca and all. And her kid."

"That kid has a name. Emily. And so, what about them?"

Alek cleared his throat. "In case you wanted to stay near them. Instead of being in the frontlines. We've got many men who can step up and help."

I shook my head. "No. I said I'll fucking handle it."

"Want backup?" Dmitri asked.

I did. And I knew just who I'd ask.

When I drove to the villa, I debated how I'd ask Becca to come with me. I owed her an explanation about the other night. It seemed like it was her fault, jumping to assumptions and accusing me of sleeping with her to get intel. I thought I wasn't in the wrong, but how would she know that? I realized she couldn't have read my mind and known that I asked about Dom ever being in her studio because I had a jealous reaction to the thought of any man in her private space. A discussion was overdue. As headstrong as she could be, I figured she'd give me that silence again.

Tying her up at a club while I scoped out the scene would be a quick way to ensure I had her full attention to hear me out. I saw now that having a steady woman in my life was a new adventure. Because of that, I counted on needing to be able to communicate in some way to avoid these kinds of disagreements.

I walked in and found her on the phone. Her expression told me enough who she was likely speaking with.

She scowled at her phone, bitter and unhappy. Pacing around the table where her phone rested, she looked cagey and impatient. Peeved.

As I walked into the great room, she glanced up at me, acknowledging me before smirking again at the phone she had on speaker.

She'd figured out how to record on her own device. Margie's phone was no longer needed to record the calls. But one glance at the device attached to her phone showed me that Murphy's call was unreachable.

How does he always know to call when I'm not here?

I realized that *all* of the calls Murphy made to Becca were when I wasn't here, and I didn't like that correlation one bit.

Was he watching to know when I was gone? I would have noticed a tail. And none of the men guarding here would be a mole and tell Murphy where I was.

Was it luck, a coincidence of timing? I'd never believed in those. Everything happened for a reason.

Did he want to get Becca on the phone alone because he would be able to reach her and manipulate her better if I wasn't here?

Wait. I narrowed my eyes as the man shouted.

"Where the fuck are you?" he demanded.

If he's asking where she is, then he can't be watching this place to know when I'm gone.

Something wasn't adding up.

So, why did he call when I was gone?

I didn't enjoy the possibility that Murphy could try to get between us.

Nothing could. I wouldn't allow it.

Becca was the one woman for me, and we damn well would be a team against the rest of the fucking world.

26

BECCA

W *hat do you want?* I wanted to scream it. I was tempted to pick up this phone and bellow that question to Steven until he just answered me.

This was how it always happened with him.

He'd call. Make demands. And hang up.

It was infuriating and unhelpful, and with the regret about the thought that I might have overreacted at the studio, lashing out at Ivan for asking about Dom again, all I cared to do was have a conversation with him where I could apologize and explain where I was coming from.

He'd started this path. Ivan was the one to initiate something more than my being a "hostage" here and feeling like a roommate.

So it was up to me to do my part and try to make it work too.

A conversation with Ivan would've been easier if he had been here, but it sounded like something was going wrong with work. With the clubs. Something. I didn't ask for details, but before he made himself scarce, he told me which clubs he'd be at or where to contact him in the city.

Another nugget of guilt came with that thought. That he was so busy because he kept driving to and from the city. I wanted to view that as a commitment, as a good thing. He wanted to be here with me. He wasn't shoving me out of the way and locking me in this house. Every night, he came here and showed up.

It left me little energy to deal with Steven calling.

"Tell me where the fuck you are."

I gritted my teeth, glancing up at Ivan striding in.

"Why?" I shot back. "Why the hell should I tell you anything?" I challenged.

"Because I'm your father, you ungrateful bitch. Because I'm your fucking father. You've never shown me any respect. You've never shown me any gratitude. Nothing."

I shook my head, smirking and bottling in my rage. The audacity. This asshole thought *he* had any grounds to deserve any respect from me? Not only that, but he also felt that I owed him thanks? For what? Neglecting me my whole life? Taking my money? Expecting me to get involved in mostly illegal shenanigans so he could profit money to keep for himself?

"Newsflash, Steven. You've got to earn respect. And you never have."

"No?" He chuckled darkly. "I haven't? Who the fuck raised you?"

"Not you."

"Who put a roof over your head?"

I fisted my hands. "Whose income went to pay for that damn roof?"

I tensed, knowing my blood pressure was sky high with another round of dealing with him. Each time he called to demand to know where I was, I worried that Ivan would suspect I was loyal to him. That by taking each call, I wanted to speak with him.

I didn't. Never again. Since he admitted to arranging to have a thug take Emily in order to get me to comply with his need for "favors", he was a dead man walking as far as I was concerned.

Ivan stood next to me, silent and watching me carefully with concern.

A glance at the phone's attachment showed that the call was still tracing. Every time Steven called, this happened. He'd rigged it to avoid being detected.

The only reason I still answered the phone was to allow Ivan and his brothers a chance to track the asshole. Otherwise, I'd never answer. I'd never speak to him again and be perfectly fine with that.

"What do you want, Steven?" I asked hotly. "What the hell do you want from me? What's going on?"

He growled. "I don't answer to you. I never will. You owe me some fucking answers."

"I don't owe you anything."

"I just need to know where you are so I can talk to you."

I raised my brows. "If I gave you a location to meet up, you'd go there just to talk to me."

Ivan watched me closely. This was the first time Steven had given me anything like a plan. Maybe this was how they could finally catch him.

"No, you stupid bitch. You're fucking that sicko. He'd just wait there to ambush me. I want to know where you are so I can make arrangements of my own to take control."

I shook my head. "I don't owe you that answer."

"You do!" he shouted. "You owe me because I am your fucking father and you should answer to me, not some stupid criminal—"

I hung up. My finger shook with the force of how badly I wanted to smash my phone or hurl it at a wall. To break it into hundreds of pieces and never have to deal with the sound of his voice ever again.

"What'd you do that for?" Ivan asked, peeved.

I growled, dropping the phone to the table. "I can't take him anymore. I'm sick to my stomach every time I hear him trying to order me around."

He frowned. "But the call wasn't traced yet."

I huffed a laugh. "They never are. Each time he calls, it's the same untraceable code on that device."

"You should have tried to keep him on the line for longer."

I shot him an angry look. "Just to subject myself to more of his verbal abuse? To listen to him rant and repeat the demands for the same thing? I haven't told him shit, and I won't."

"But he might have slipped. He could've lost his temper or patience and mentioned something that could be a clue."

I shook my head. "I doubt it. He's been at this conning game for a long time now. He won't reveal anything unless it'd help himself."

"I beg to differ. Everyone fucks up sometime, sooner or later."

I eyed him, wondering if he was referring to me, too. That I'd fucked up in accusing him of sleeping with me for bad reasons.

"Whatever." I shrugged, raw and worn out from dealing with Steven to want to bicker with Ivan. Butting heads and quarreling was fine with him. It made our interactions that much more interesting and challenging. A push-and-pull balance.

But not now. I'd been so excited to see him to own up and apologize for what I said the other night, but all I wanted was to relax instead.

Live to fight another day.

"I've asked Margie to handle Emily tonight."

Of all the things he could've said, that was the last thing I expected. "What?"

He nodded. "You heard me."

He wasn't the sort of man to repeat himself. I should've felt pissed that he was trying to call the shots where Emily was concerned. He'd admitted that he wanted to see himself as a father figure for her, but it wasn't cool for him to override *my* choices about her as her only current and actual parent.

"Why?"

"Because you and I are going out."

I gawked at him, sure that I was hearing things. He wanted to take me out? Tonight? I didn't know why. "Like… on a date?" I was excited, but also iffy about it. I'd been feeling more tired than usual lately. A quiet night in with just him would be sweet, but I doubted that would interest him.

He nodded. "We're going out."

"What's the occasion?" I licked my lips, letting the idea of spending quality alone time with him fill my hopelessly romantic heart. "Is there an occasion?"

He shook his head. "No. I want you with me."

Okay...

"And I don't like how Steven seems to be aware of the best times to reach you."

I furrowed my brow. "Huh?" I didn't pay too much attention to the timing of his calls. Any and every time he called, it was a bad one.

"You haven't noticed that he always calls when I'm not here?"

Well, that shut me up. I hadn't noticed that. Maybe because I'd fallen into the habit of recording the calls, I knew Ivan wouldn't miss out on the messages.

"He calls when I'm not here with you. It's making me wonder if he knows when we're apart. And how."

I pointed at myself. "Are you accusing me of sharing the information of your whereabouts with him?"

He growled and rolled his eyes. "No. Stop taking *everything* I say as an attack."

I do that. Dammit. I hadn't realized I was doing that.

I couldn't help but be on guard and suspicious. I always was. How could I not be with the life I've had? But I didn't need to use it against Ivan all the time. He was trusting me, and I could show him the same.

"He calls when I'm not here, and that makes me uncomfortable." He stepped closer, cupping my face and gazing down at me calmly. "I know you're not telling him anything. I got the impression you wouldn't from the first time he called and you were open with me to want to hurry and record it as evidence for me to share with my brothers."

I nodded, sighing and letting some of the stress leak from me. Any time he touched me at all, his contact soothed the anxiety deep in my soul.

"I don't want to know why he contacts you like that. I'd prefer it if he didn't at all." He stroked his thumb over my cheek. "I wish he'd man up and just fucking come out of hiding once and for all so I could remove one pain in the ass from the face of the earth."

"I know."

"But it makes me uneasy to know he's trying to butt in between us, calling you when I'm not here."

"And that's why you want to take me out tonight?"

"Not the only reason." He almost smiled.

"What are the other reasons?"

He lifted one shoulder and let it fall as he stepped back, releasing me from his touch. "You'll see."

Excitement and nervousness melded into one chaotic sensation.

I'd never really gone on a proper date before. The two boyfriends I'd had in the past were workaholics like me, never having money or time to take me out and show me a night of fun and affection.

Dom wined and dined me, but that had all been a long-lasting manipulation.

Leave it to the Mafia man to know how to treat a woman. To plan to treat me.

A smile threatened to break across my face, but I kept it in. I didn't want to seem too eager and easy. I still needed to apologize for how I'd spoken to him the other night. Until I had that off my chest, I would feel uneasy. If any kind of a future was in store for us, I wanted to enter it with a clear conscience and being able to admit my flaws.

And if our future would consist of actually spending time together alone—on real dates—I wanted the rest of our lives to start now.

Me and him. For good. No matter how complicated everything seemed to be before we could get together like this and be on the same page.

"Like I said, I've arranged things with Margie. Emily is in good hands." He arched one brow at me. "Now go on. Get ready to leave with me."

I bit my lip and nodded, curious what he had in mind.

27

IVAN

We arrived at the club the Valkov Bratva used to own. Not much had changed. The building was obviously the same. While the new owners had changed some décor, the premise was the same.

Nik suggested going undercover, and that was a valid idea, but I hadn't needed to try to do that tonight. I recognized no one here. The crowd of guests seemed new, and I felt the chances were slim that I would be recognized.

Becca stuck with me, clinging to me. Her eyes were wide open as she took in the people dressed in few garments, or nothing at all.

"So, this wasn't exactly what I was thinking of when you said you wanted to take me out..."

I grinned at her, scoping out the people milling around near the bar. "Sorry."

She smirked up at me. "Is this for pleasure? Or business? Or...?"

"My vanilla good girl," I teased.

She sighed against me as I hugged her, looking over her head and staying alert.

"Would you be okay if I said I'd brought you here for pleasure only?"

She licked her lips, watching a man eat out a woman across the room. "If I stay with you. And you... uh, ease me into all of this."

Just like that, she made me happy. A willingness to try. An openness to compromise. I'd hit gold in finding her.

"It's both. I'm here to check things out for the Bratva. But once that's done, I intend to get a room and spend some time with you."

She shivered, and I watched her skin break out in goosebumps. I hadn't told her what to wear, but the simple, short black dress she'd chosen was fine. With skinny straps and a low cut, she showed me ample flesh, but she was still overdressed compared to the others.

"How does that sound?" I asked her before pressing a soft kiss to her shoulder.

She laughed once. "Hey, you're the boss."

I loved that she'd put that faith in me, comfortable with my being in charge.

Over the next couple of hours, we walked around. Both of us had a couple of drinks, but we weren't drunk by any means. Becca's role was to be my guest, my partner, my woman. And she did that splendidly. She watched scenes. She asked me questions. All the while, I acted casual, like this was any other ordinary night for me at a club, waiting to fuck my beautiful woman.

Nothing was happening. Plenty of sexual acts were carried out. Many scenes were performed. But I noticed not a single hint of drugs being sold, handed out, bought, or taken. Nothing at all.

In all honesty, it seemed like a slow night. The guests weren't rowdy. No one wanted to fight or cause a brawl. The guards and floor monitors were easygoing and not seeming stressed about anything.

As the night wore on, I worried that I was wasting my time here. That my idea to check things out here was a stupid plan. If something happened at another club, especially one under the Valkov ownership, I'd be pissed.

After watching and realizing no bad activities were waiting to happen here, I lightened up and paid more attention to Becca.

She'd been so curious and intrigued all evening. Watching and smiling at the scenes, then sometimes wincing and furrowing her brow at the more intense ones.

She grimaced at the idea of anything to do with anal, but that didn't surprise me. That took some warming up to, and I honestly didn't care for it. I would do whatever Becca needed or wanted from me, but if she wasn't a fan of trying anal, that was fine by me.

What pleased me most was how she appeared most aroused when watching a woman tied up or spanked. A flogger might be too much yet, but I appreciated her body's honest reaction to the sorts of things I liked.

"Come with me," I told her once I signaled that I'd like a room with her.

For the sake of not letting anyone see me and recognize me, I closed the wall to the windows.

Becca walked around the dimly lit room, circling the massive bed in the center.

"How, uh, how does this work?" she asked timidly.

I stalked over to her and cupped her face, kissing her hard.

"Like this."

I was too excited and feral for her to take this slow. In my mind, I rehearsed a long, drawn out scene of teasing and taunting. Of prolonging her buildup to come. That slow approach flew out the window.

Just seeing her in here, trusting me and putting her faith in me to be at a club like this pushed me to fuck her right now.

"Oh!" She squeaked, caught by surprise as I walked her to the bed and followed her down. As she reached up and clung to me, keeping me close, she kissed me back just as hard, ready to share a special night with me.

"And like this," I said, standing to yank her dress off and lose my pants. I wouldn't last long myself, but before things got too hot and heated, I had to explain myself.

"The other night, at your studio—"

She groaned, pouting as she helped shimmy out of her bra and panties. "I'm sorry. I shouldn't have been so harsh and said those things to you."

I removed the last of my clothes, walking toward the shelf with the cuffs. "And I realize how you assumed what you did when I asked about Dom right afterward. I only did because I was jealous."

"Jealous?" She tried to sit up on the bed, but she slumped down and rolled to her stomach under my prompting as she let me cuff her wrist to one post.

"Yes. That he could have been there with you, alone."

She shook her head. "He wasn't."

I cuffed her ankle to another post. "And I knew that, but I wanted to hear you say it again. I don't like the idea of any other man being there."

She smiled, watching as I moved to lock her other ankle up. Her nipples pointed out, hard buds I wanted to pinch. Her pussy shone with her juices dripping out. And she wasn't all the way tied yet.

I growled, trying to pace myself as I secured her ankle, making her lie flat, then went to her other hand and cuffed it.

"I want to be the only one to be there with you in a place you deem your special sanctuary." I climbed on the bed, angling her to lift to her knees. As soon as I had her ass in the air, I dragged my tongue from her clit to her taint, licking her cream in one long, hot stroke.

"Oh, fuck."

I slapped her ass. "Louder."

She gasped, and I grinned as her cheek turned red from my hit.

Again, I licked her, and she cried out.

"I said louder." I smacked her other ass cheek, fingering her as she dripped more.

"Oh..." She moaned, a husky sound of pure need.

I kissed her ass, brushing my lips over the raised flesh I'd slapped, feeling the warmth rising up to the surface as goosebumps spread out. I didn't stop fingering her, stretching her velvety walls.

"More, Ivan. More."

And I gave her exactly what she begged for. Alternating between spanking her and licking her, I pushed her close to an orgasm. Precum dripped from my tip, smearing on the bed sheet, but I refused to slam into her until she came at least once.

She gave me two. Sucking on her clit while fingering her got her to come first. Then as I spanked her ass and pinched her clit, she came again.

I was about to explode. I couldn't wait any longer. When I gave up, shoving my aching cock deep into her, I reveled in her screams.

For more. To spank her. To pummel her pussy. Hearing her loosen up to talk so dirty goaded me to take her even harder, and I knew it wouldn't be long before I could introduce more kinks.

For now, this was perfect. She was perfect. Her hands fisted as the cuffs dug into her, keeping her locked. Trapped and lax in my restraints, she took the brutal pounding and cried out for more.

Together, we came in a sweaty mess. Tangled together as I slumped over her, spent and sated, I felt the fading flutters of her pussy clenching my dick and sucking it deeper into her heat.

I didn't speak. She focused on nothing but breathing as steadily as possible. No words were necessary. I'd learned my lesson about not speaking up. We had to maintain communication to work, and we'd achieved that.

We'd cleared that air from how the other night ended.

And now, we could only look forward to what could lie ahead.

After I uncuffed her, I cleaned her up and checked that her ass wasn't too raw from the spankings. All she wanted was my touch, though, and I had no qualms or hesitations about lying with her and cuddling her, kissing her as I wanted. Tenderly on her lips. Softly on her cheeks. Gently on her brow. I wished for her to understand that while I could be hard and rough, I would never give up a chance to dote on her and shower her with delicate caresses. She would never miss out on aftercare with me. Never.

"About that other night," she said, speaking up after a long while of relaxing. "I want you to know that I feel the same."

I nodded, kissing her deeply.

"I want you so much it hurts. And I know I might not be the sort of woman you're used to." She gestured at the room before returning her hand to my face, stroking softly.

I grunted, running my hand over her waist, then her ass. "I think you're not giving yourself enough credit."

She smiled. "I want you to understand that I'm willing to be the woman you need and want."

I cleared my throat, scooting closer to her as we lay facing each other. "Did you enjoy what we did tonight?"

She nodded. "It's a good start."

Start? Fuck, I love her.

"And I'm excited to see what else you'll teach me."

I kissed her hard, pulling her to lie over me and straddle me.

You're teaching me more, sweetheart. How to love. How good it feels to find love.

I never thought I'd settle. I never imagined actually finding a woman who would like me for who I was.

She hadn't been a pawn or a hostage for a long while. Instead, she was the perfect woman for me, accepting my darkness and wanting me regardless.

No, not accepting, but embracing and welcoming.

Becca wasn't so shy that she couldn't adjust to what I liked, and I wasn't so stupid as to take her for granted and anticipate that she might prefer things simple and vanilla sometimes too. And that was just what we'd figure out as we went along with this.

Because she was a treasure I refused to ever risk losing.

28

BECCA

Ivan held my hand as we left the room where he'd spanked me and fucked me so well I wished we never had to leave. Of course, I didn't mean that. Emily was waiting for me. For us.

But it was nice to have that separation. That at the house, we could be more like a family. Two adults—or three, including Margie—to handle one baby. For now. At this club, though, I felt freer to shed my responsibilities and trust in Ivan to steer me to pleasure. Under his control, I could simply be and know that he'd catch me after I fell. It was a liberating feeling, one I wished to repeat as soon as possible.

"What if you move in?" he asked.

I smiled up at me. "Didn't... we sort of already do that?"

He smirked. "Into my room."

I nodded.

"So long as you can be a little more quiet at night when Emily is sleeping."

"I can't guarantee it."

He squeezed my fingers tighter, and I leaned against him, loving that I could be this woman at his side. That he'd chosen *me* out of all the women in the world.

"But after Murphy's dead..."

I didn't listen to whatever he might have said. All my senses faded as I locked eyes on a couple of men I recognized. Sounds ceased to filter through my ears. Everything burned down to tunnel vision as I stared at the men over on the other side of the room. My body felt numb and immobile, but my heart raced like I was actively finishing a marathon.

"Becca?" Ivan's fingers gripped mine tighter once more, jarring me from the shock and fear that washed over me.

"Those men," I whispered.

The guys turned at just that moment, as if my hissed words floated to them from across this lobby space. One smirked. The other narrowed his eyes. We'd made eye contact, and I didn't like the implications of seeing them here. They hadn't been here when Ivan and I walked around, when he kept his eyes on the activity here.

These two were men I remembered from my days with Dominic. Rossinis.

The men Ivan and his Bratva considered enemies. Between Steven and these Italians, something was in the works, and I didn't want to know what it meant.

"Fuck." Ivan reached for his phone, but before he could bring it to his ear and make a call, the doors up front opened. Men rushed in. All of them wore uniforms. Behind them were others with guns raised, the undercover cops or detectives.

They swarmed in so suddenly that it took the DJ or person in charge of the music a full stop to cut off the noise. Shouts and screams sounded instead. Panic filled the room as guests and staff ran to leave.

I couldn't tear my gaze from the Rossinis over there, noticing that they hadn't budged. Unflinching and cool, they stared at me expectantly.

Did they know Ivan was here? Did Steven? Or that *I* was? Questions ping-ponged in my head so fast that I felt dizzy. If not for Ivan's strong hand in mind, I would've fallen due to my shaking knees.

"Ivan? What's going on?"

He gritted his teeth, noticing the Rossinis.

They weren't just the enemy. They recognized me. The sensation that they could be here *for* me was such a horrid one, I couldn't shake it. I never wanted to be involved in any Mafia matters, and I felt like I was trapped in something now.

"It's staged," Ivan hissed. "The Rossinis, the cops. They set it up to be ambushed."

"Is this one of the Bratva's places?" I asked, pressing up closer to him as people moved so fast to escape.

Then someone fell.

Another.

In the corner, a woman dropped to the floor, having a seizure.

"What is going on?" I couldn't keep the hysteria out of my voice.

"The drugs," Ivan snapped. "They're distributing the fucking drugs here."

"What drugs?"

"You!" A cop zeroed in on Ivan and marched over. "He's the owner."

"I'm not." Ivan stood straighter, unafraid of the officer. "This establishment is no longer part of my family's business profile."

"Yeah, yeah. Fancy words I don't give a fuck about. You're here just like the tip claimed." He jerked his thumb toward the cops helping the people who'd fallen.

Chaos ensued as another club guest fell, clutching their neck.

Ivan shook his head, holding on tight to me. "You've got it wrong," he insisted to the cop. Another one approached, seeming ready to cuff him. From the side, men hurried closer. I recognized them as some of the guards at the vacation villa. I hadn't realized they'd been here all along, but of course they would've been here as backup. Ivan wasn't stupid. He likely had security all the time.

As they came closer, I was pushed back. Tightening my fingers on Ivan's, I gripped hard and fought not to be separated from him.

He turned, glaring in my direction with the determination to keep me with him in this frenzied crowd. His arm lifted, and a cop reached out to cuff him. The metal didn't lock on his wrist, and I felt safe as I felt his hand taking mine.

Or not.

Someone else had wrestled closer, and it was a stranger who gripped my hand and pulled me back.

"Ivan!"

He lunged after me, his face set in stony fury, but too much was happening. The cops went for him. The Bratva guards interfered. Other club members and guests rushed between us.

Before I could inhale another deep breath to scream for him again, strong arms locked around me. They hauled me outside, strapping tape over my mouth as they steered me into a car waiting in the alley.

A sickening sense of déjà vu hit me. Not again. Not like this. When Ivan took me out of that club, I ended up learning love and lust, pleasure and passion. Those things would only ever make sense with him. And that was why I kicked and flailed so hard that the men dropped me. Pain radiated up from my tailbone at the impact. My ass was still sore from Ivan's spankings, but this sudden plummet to the floor stung bad.

It knocked the breath out of me. I lost precious seconds to scramble to my feet and run away. To run to Ivan.

They caught me in their arms again, and the Rossinis tossed me into the back of a car.

On the ride, I bucked and fought, resisting the zip ties on my wrists in front of me. No matter how much I tugged awkwardly at the tape over my mouth and sticking far back into my hair, I couldn't rip it off.

I wasn't back there for long, stunned and shocked with fear and anger. I didn't have ample time to plan or pay attention to many details, determined to yank this tape off, then bite at the zip ties. Anything. Something. I'd give it my all to escape and retaliate because I had too much to fight for now.

Ivan. Emily. Hell, even Margie. Whatever these Rossinis wanted, they wouldn't win. If they were working with Steven, I'd kill him myself. For once in my life, I had a bright, grand future to look forward to. And I'd do anything to get back to my man and know it would still happen.

The men weren't gentle removing me from the car, and their

hands locked down on my upper arms to the point of bruising pain as they led me into a building. They'd parked in an underground parking garage, and I was deprived of seeing what structure they'd driven me to. I was aware that I needed to notice and remember all the details, but my sense of staying alert had gone haywire. Everything passed in a blur of too many things to see and track.

Once they pushed me into a room, something bare but functional like an interview room, I zeroed in on something I could easily remember. Someone I so readily recognized.

Dominic.

He sat on the other side of a fold-up table, distinguished as ever, his graying hair slicked back perfectly, his manicured nails neat and even as he folded his hands together on the surface. That smug smile was the same, his dark, beady eyes just I remembered. Dressed in an impeccable suit, he watched me as his friends shoved me into a chair across from him.

My ass stung. The fall to the floor made my tailbone ache more. But it was nothing compared to the stinging agony of them ripping the tape off and yanking out hair with it.

I breathed hard through it, growling and glowering at Dominic.

No cops were in here.

Just him.

He had the control here, and I hated it. Men always lorded over me, but I wanted to reset things back to where I could surrender to Ivan and know he would protect me and care for me while he was in control.

Dominic cleared his throat, betraying no emotions with his lack of expression. "I'd like to speak with you about your artwork."

I sat there, still, letting his words replay through my mind. Then again. And again. No matter how many times I tried to understand them, they didn't fit.

I lost it. Cracking up so hard that my eyes watered, I curled over and laughed. And laughed.

"You *what?*"

Now, of all fucking times, he wanted to talk about my artwork?

Now? Was he insane? He'd taken me to Europe to "sponsor" my artwork without ever seeming to realize I was a fan of the Impressionist style, not Minimalist. Or that I sculpture bare pieces without paint. Or that I was even a multimedia artist at all.

Was this a joke? A mockery? A fucking game? I felt like I was going insane after he'd so coolly told me the very last thing I'd ever expected to hear. I'd never counted on seeing him again, and certainly never like this—after he'd sent his thugs to kidnap me from a damn sex club.

"My *artwork?*" I shook my head. "You don't fucking care. You never cared. You pretended to be interested in my artwork just to keep me close and keep tabs on Steven somehow." Chuckling, I tried to calm down.

Laughing at him wasn't the smart reaction, though. He snapped, perhaps thinking I was making fun of him.

Standing up quickly, he shoved his chair back and thrust his arm over the table, pointing a knife at me.

"You took something of mine," he seethed, baring his teeth. "And I want it back."

I swallowed, sobering up with the real and present danger of a weapon that close to me. "I…" I shook my head, determined not to look scared, but mad. Not terrified, but furious and bold. "I didn't take a damn thing from you."

Just your child. I debated whether he knew about Emily.

"Your father took something of mine, and I want it back."

Steven! It was always about him. If he'd used me somehow while I was with Dominic…

I clenched my teeth, breathing through my nose to try to stay level-headed. "I do not associate with Steven. I never have. And I never will." I was sick of everyone assuming I was his accomplice just because we were related by blood.

"You stupid idiot." He stood straighter, gesturing for his men to grab me again. "You won't beat me. He won't win. I want it back, and I *will* get it."

Emily? No. He couldn't mean her. If Dom wanted something

Steven took from me, he couldn't mean how Steven tried to get Emily taken that same night Ivan captured me.

I tried to understand. As the men pulled me off the chair, I scrambled to solve it all and figure out why Dominic expected anything from *me*.

If he's coming for Emily...

I clung to the knowledge that Ivan wouldn't let Dominic—anyone —near my baby.

He'd keep her safe.

All I had to do was try to do the same for myself until I could run from the predicament I'd fallen into.

29

IVAN

"Get your fucking hands off me." I shoved the cop back, searching for Becca.

She'd been right there. Next to me. Scared and nervous.

In the melee of all the club guests running, the staff workers arguing with the cops, the officers swarming and trying to arrest any Mafia person they saw—except that pair of Rossinis—it was chaos.

Even when the lights came on and the music was silenced, it was hard to follow the rushed frenzy of it all.

Once the cops noticed more of the people dropping like flies, all drugged, they shifted their focus to them and less on me. My soldiers and guards stood between me and the fuckers trying to arrest me.

They had no grounds. I didn't have any drugs. I was no longer a supervisor of this establishment and my family no longer owned it.

"Becca!" I tried to shout for her again, spinning and enraged to find her.

"They took her," a Bratva soldier reported, rushing in from the door leading to the exit. "They drove off."

"Fuck!" I ran out with him, desperate to get in my car and drive.

As soon as I got in the driver's seat, Maxim called.

"What?" I snapped. He was the one who operated the tracking software that synced with the tiny tab I'd put on Becca's necklace. He was the brother I wanted to call, but I didn't want to know why he was reaching out to me first.

"Get out of that club. I got intel that they're staging a—"

"Too fucking late," I barked.

"The cops showed?"

"Yes. And someone took Becca."

He swore, and the sound of typing came from his end. "I'll find her. In the meantime, though, I've got news. Fucking finally. Nik had to make a few calls to the right people."

"Fill me in." I didn't care who got the intel. I'd use it. And I would find Becca. I refused to consider the possibility that I wouldn't. She belonged at my side. She should be with me forever. I didn't find her just to lose her.

In the meantime, I was all ears for whatever would help me bring those fuckers down.

"Those drugs are experiments gone wrong. My sources say they originated in labs in Amsterdam, but someone else got their hands on it."

"The Rossinis?" I guessed as I drove away from the club, waiting for Becca's location.

"Yes. The Rossinis bought them for the use of a weapon, but others within their organization wanted to use them as ways to get customers to get hooked on elite drugs."

Always about the money.

"Murphy was one of the first ones who found out about them, though. He learned about them on the black market," Maxim explained, "but he couldn't circulate them on his own and reap all the money and take all the cuts for it himself."

I nodded. "Yeah, because he's supposed to be a cop and would need to use criminal means to move them."

"Hence, the Rossinis. He approached Dominic Rossini, who was skeptical of the product. The Rossinis were interested, and Dom wanted to look into it, but Murphy was too secretive about it all."

I grunted. "That's probably the phone call Becca overheard. About the long-term project Dom wanted to do with Murphy."

"I think so too. Murphy, according to the skeptics from the Rossini side, wanted to get rich on the drugs and pin the circulation of it on us, on our Bratva. That was the incentive to the Rossinis, to use us as the scapegoat for the drugs appearing here."

Which explains why they had them at the club we recently sold. Somewhere they must have thought we still operated.

"The Rossinis had too many things to worry about, though, for Dom to focus on this agreement. Their infighting, for starters. They were interested in a scheme to hurt the Bratva, but Murphy was too pushy."

"I can't wait to kill that fucker."

"Agreed. Murphy started having people plant the drugs in sex clubs when you weren't there. I think that's why he wanted to know where you were when he called Becca. He must have realized that your taking Becca was a way to track you through her. Then he'd have his lackeys plant the drugs when we weren't looking."

It was a diversion, just like I'd thought, but I didn't see how Murphy was keeping this up.

"The one detail I can't understand is how the drugs got here, though. My sources seem to think Dom had the drugs with him, on Rossini property, and Murphy was bitter with him because Dom wouldn't release them to him yet."

"And that's likely why he wanted to string Becca along, as insurance of some kind."

Maxim sighed. "I think so too. But if Dom wasn't interested in the plan yet, and sent Becca packing when he seemed to call off the plans with Murphy in that last phone call that she overheard, how are the drugs getting here? Murphy's got to have a supply here somehow."

"Maybe he bought some and had it on hand to distribute."

"Okay, but he's got to maintain the supply for his plan to work. A few people being drugged isn't newsworthy. Dozens of them is. That's what I'm trying to figure out. Where Murphy's supply is."

"And if I find that supply, I'd find him," I added.

"Better yet, you could find him and kill him before he circulates any more of the drugs and causes trouble for the Bratva."

As if I needed any more incentive to kill Steven Murphy. He was already a dead man. So were the fuckers who'd taken Becca tonight.

With every minute that she wasn't with me, next to me in the passenger seat and proving that love could exist for me, that a bond could build and grow between opposites like us, I burned with a furious need to inflict pain and death. I became unhinged, driven to slaughter them all.

"Where is she?" I demanded.

"Sorry. It took a while to start up and search."

Still, he didn't continue.

"Please, Maxim. Please." I didn't care if the desperation was evident.

"She never takes the necklace off, right?"

She better not have. I tensed, wondering if someone could have swept her and checked for bugs or trackers. "Not since I've known her."

"I'm looking. I swear, I'm looking. She might be somewhere that it's hard to reach. In a basement or something."

I'm coming for you, sweetheart. I swear I am.

"Call me as soon as you have a location." After he said he would, I called the house and asked Margie to stay in Emily's room. Just in case. Then I spoke with the guards at the villa, letting them know what happened.

They all jumped to action, promising to do as I asked.

Alek called too, telling me he was on his way to help me, to be backup.

And still, I waited for direction from Maxim, hopeful that he'd be able to steer me which way to go to get my girl.

I found her once. No matter the danger and complications from the fucking Italians and the crookedest cop, I'd find her again.

Then keep her forever.

BECCA

ominic's men stopped behind a familiar building. Back here, it looked like any other building along this alleyway. The front, though, had large windows for passersby to peer through and get peeks of a variety of artwork.

It felt like a lifetime had passed since I was last here. The art gallery where Morgan was the star. Where all I was allotted was a tiny thumbnail image on the pamphlet and a one-liner about me.

The art gallery where Steven called and asked me to retrieve an envelope for him and I'd refused. When I had those fanciful dreams of a man loving me and protecting me.

I'd found one, despite the hell I'd endured from the rapist forcing me to enter the back door.

Ivan. I missed him and wished he could be here to kill Dominic like he'd promised he would.

I stumbled on a step, breathless and so confused as Dominic growled and pushed me into the empty gallery. Lights remained off, and one of these thugs must have canceled the alarm.

In the middle of the floor space, I stood alone and nervous.

"What's going on?"

Dominic held his left hand out, gesturing at one of his men to give him something. In his right hand, he gripped that knife. "Which pieces of shit are yours?" he snarled at me as he accepted a small sledge-hammer from his man.

I tensed, hunching my shoulders as he slammed the hammer into another artist's sculpture. Shards went flying, scattering over the floor like he'd beaten a clay piñata.

He didn't even know which pieces were mine. That was how little he'd paid attention or cared when he strung me along.

"Which ones!" He didn't wait for my reply, smashing the hammer on every sculpture in the room. His chest heaved from the exertion, growling with his labored breaths as he stalked around the room. Rossini thugs hurried to pick through the debris, and I watched them before Dominic turned to using the knife.

I was too confused to be wounded by the destruction of my artwork. I could make more. I *would* make more. What remained fore-front in my mind was *why*. Had he gone crazy? Deranged?

What can he want back that would be in—

I stifled a gasp as it clicked.

Zoning out as he moved to the paintings, slicing his knife through the canvas then checking the edge where the artwork connected to the frame, I knew.

I figured it out with his rampant destruction of all these pieces. He didn't need to destroy the others, but I was so stunned that I couldn't speak. I was so shocked that I couldn't point out which ones were mine.

Because he was after my artwork. He was convinced I'd taken them back home with something of his inside them.

Smuggling.

That had to be it. This plan with Steven. I had been nothing but a pawn in it all, a vessel for them to smuggle drugs here. I recalled enough Italian to understand the Rossini ordering his fellow thug to look for them in the mess. Vials. Envelopes. Thin packages. All believed to be hidden within the artwork.

Oh, my God.

I felt disoriented, unable to draw in a deep breath as the truth settled upon me.

I'd been used so horribly in all this. All that time Dom had transported my artwork throughout Europe, he'd been hiding and stashing drugs in my artwork throughout it all. I doubted he personally had done it. If he had, he'd know which pieces were the Trojan horses. Someone he employed had to have arranged it.

Steven wanted those drugs. Dom did too. The long-term plan had gone sour, though, and now it was a race to find the evidence.

Oh. My. God.

I struggled with this realization, so thrown off by how I could have ever gotten mixed in with all this.

No wonder Dom was so eager to convince me to travel with him. No wonder he insisted on bringing my artwork and convincing me to spend all that time away from home.

And Steven. He'd known about it too, never once considering doing the right thing of warning his daughter that a crime lord was using her to smuggle drugs.

That had to be why he'd wanted me to get an envelope for him at one of those sex clubs. Payment, I bet, for these drugs. These very same drugs that likely caused those guests to fall and struggle when the cops ambushed them.

"How..." I found my voice, confused and eager to understand. "How did you know I was at that club tonight?"

Another Rossini spoke up, scowling at me as he picked through the debris from torn canvases and busted frames from Dominic's enraged ruination. "We didn't. We were there handing out the drugs to see if your father would show up, mad that we were overriding his product."

"We happened to be there, and there you were," the other man said, one of the two I'd seen at the club, "the answer to all our problems."

"Not so fast," Dominic shouted. He hurried toward me, fuming as he smashed more paintings down. "We still haven't found those drugs, and I'll be damned if your fucking father beats me to them."

I panted, frantic to breathe steadily during the intense rush of adrenaline and fear. As he neared me, I cowered back. The need to puke returned. And my God, I was going to faint.

I blinked, thinking through the overwhelming sensations that claimed me.

I'd felt them before.

This wasn't only lightheadedness from being scared.

I'm... pregnant?

I lowered my hand to my belly, thinking back. I'd felt like this when I was pregnant with Emily. Just slightly out of breath enough that I noticed. And the on and off nausea, never so bad that it stopped me from being functional, but appearing suddenly when it came.

Oh, my God!

I recalled the last period I'd had, well before I met Ivan. I'd missed my monthly, but I'd dismissed it as a bodily reaction to all the stress of the last month and a half.

Of all times. I couldn't believe it. Of all times to realize this, now, when I was in danger. Right this minute, when the deranged crime lord who'd raped me wanted to find illegal drugs he'd had hidden in my artwork.

Ivan. He'd knocked me up, likely from that first night he'd taken me.

Of all the times to learn that I'm carrying his child! It seemed so incredulous that I struggled to accept it as a fact. I hadn't taken a test, but I *felt* it. It was just like what I experienced before.

But right now, when I could really help Ivan with this Mafia war, this vendetta against Steven, I was unable to reach him or contact him for help.

Just stall him. Stay safe and alive. Cooperate. And stall him.

Because Ivan had to care too much not to chase me down. Somehow, he had to find me. I willed it to be true.

Dominic returned to me, walking lopsidedly and tired from the exertion of winging that sledgehammer up and down to pulverize the sculptures, then slicing and smashing the paintings.

Breathing hard, looking every bit the diabolical maniac he was, he glared directly at me.

"Where is the rest of it? Tell me where the rest of your artwork is that I showed them in Italy."

I bit my lip so he wouldn't see it tremble. I had to remain strong. I would be strong. There was no other choice.

Stall him. Cooperate. And pray Ivan will know how to find me. It was that or I wait for a chance to run away. As soon as I could—safely, since I wasn't running for just my safety but also my baby's—I would.

"Back there," I said, wishing my voice were stronger as I pointed to the rear storage room.

He lifted the knife and aimed it at me. "Lead the way."

31

IVAN

Maxim called with Becca's location as soon as Alek met up with me.

He jumped in the passenger seat, confused when the address led to an art gallery. "What the fuck?"

I wasn't questioning it. I pressed the pedal down and sped in that direction.

"Send backup," Alek ordered. "But have them keep their distance."

I smirked at my oldest brother, grateful for his help but wondering why he personally came with me. Since he'd taken over as the *Pakhan*, he'd struggled with stepping back and not being in action. This had to be another one of those times, and I'd roll with it.

"Why an art gallery?" he asked.

"Because she's an artist," I guessed.

"But it's closed," Alek said.

I shook my head as we neared it. "And normal operating business hours have stopped us before?"

I parked further from the building so I wouldn't tip anyone off inside. She had to be here. I resisted the thought of her necklace being here, but not the woman I loved.

My desperation to save her scaled higher with every step I took jogging closer. Caught in a mix of anger and calm, I tried to bank on the anticipation of killing the motherfuckers who took her and letting that bloodshed wash away this hellacious agony of worrying about losing her. Only when they ceased to live would my world be tilted back on its axis like it should be.

Alek hadn't lost his street smarts since taking over the Bratva leadership. He crept along with me in the shadows, still just as much of an expert at sneaking and spying on the enemy.

Side by side, we peered through the windows and watched.

Becca!

She was alive, if scared. Standing in the center of the gallery space, she wrung her hands together and flinched each time a tall man smashed a sculpture.

"Dominic," Alek said, glancing around to see our Bratva men killing Rossini guards stationed out front. We worked as a team, and I would never forget that.

"That's Dominic?" I asked, seeing the man in the flesh for the first time. Laying my eyes on Becca's rapist had me itching to wrench these locked doors open and kill him with my bare hands.

"Yes. What the fuck is he doing?"

We watched as the man smashed and sliced all the artwork. I had no clue why, but I kept my focus on Becca more than anything. She was terrified, but standing strong. Nervous, but not hiding.

My sweetheart. So strong and determined to survive.

"Are you going to be okay with stepping in as a father to another man's child?" Alek asked.

The question seemed ridiculous, given what we were doing. This wasn't an idle time to chat. He had to be plotting and scoping the surroundings for how we could best get in there and save Becca.

But he asked me that, of all things? Right now?

"What?" I snapped.

"I see how you look at her."

"With determination to get her out of there and kill that fucker?"

He nodded, still watching through the windows. "You are in love with her."

I grunted. "Didn't I just say that?"

"You love her?"

I wouldn't deny it. I couldn't. After the deep intimacy we shared earlier tonight, I had no doubt in my mind that Becca was the one woman for me, the perfect partner I hadn't realized I'd been waiting for.

"Of course, I'd be a father to Emily." I glanced at him, annoyed that he wanted to have this sentimental, let's-talk-about-feelings crap right now. "It doesn't matter whose sperm made her. She's a baby. Innocent."

Alek nodded. "Good. I just wanted to check."

Shitty timing, though.

"So, how do you want to do this?"

There was no chance of breaking in from the front. The wide windows would give us away too soon.

I tipped my head to the side, indicating that we should go around to the back.

I'm coming for you, sweetheart.

I hated to lose sight of her, but it was only temporary. As soon as we rounded to the back and snuck in, I'd see her again and save her. Dominic was a dead man.

Leaving Alek out front might have been a good idea, to maintain a view of her, but he wouldn't have been able to break in himself if things turned for the worse. Besides, he was my boss, the Bratva's *Pakhan*, and my beloved brother. I couldn't leave him out here unprotected.

Together, we snuck to the back of the building. Bratva men were just finishing killing the Rossini guards out there, but it didn't seem like they'd snuck in the back door yet.

Alek and I did, finding the enemy who'd started this all.

I held up my hand to stop Alek from shooting at Murphy.

After all the bullshit he'd put us through, hiding and staying untouchable while out of sight.

After all the abuse and neglect he'd done to Becca over her whole life.

Here he was, a pathetic piece of shit tearing through paintings, just like Dominic had been doing in the gallery space out front.

I'd been waiting for this moment, the sweet mark of time where I could end his life.

But he spun, noticing us and sneering. "Fuck off."

Alek and I rushed at him together, stopping him from firing his gun at us. We were younger, fitter, and faster, and he'd never have a chance to overpower us up close. I hadn't wanted him to fire his gun yet. The sound would've alerted Dominic and his men in the other, bigger gallery, and I didn't want them to react and fire around Becca.

As Alek and I secured the crooked cop who thrashed and fought to get free, we were joined by Dom and Becca.

"You motherfucker!" Dom pushed Becca further into the room. His gun was aimed at her head, but when he spotted Murphy, he switched to aiming at him.

I grabbed Alek to pull him back, and Murphy lifted his gun to point at Dom.

Becca stared at me, hands up and eyes wide as she started to angle away from Dom.

He noticed, not taking his eyes off Murphy. "Stop. Stop right where you are," he ordered her.

She stiffened, stopping in her tracks.

I licked my lips, staring at her and willing her to understand that I would not let her down. With all the weapons in here, all the anger directed every which way, I would not fail her.

Because I love you. So fucking much. The suspense killed me, squeezing my heart and making my head ache. I was overwhelmed with the urge to run to her and bring her to safety.

Alek's grip on my sleeve stopped me from moving as we waited to see who'd shoot first.

"You lying motherfucker," Dom repeated, lashing out at Murphy. "You changed the plans for the drugs."

"I didn't change anything," Murphy scowled. "I just decided to start acting on the plan. You were taking too long, so I started selling what I had on hand from the first batch."

Dom locked his arm, growling as he held the gun higher. "That's bullshit!"

"You weren't moving fast enough," Murphy argued. "There was money to be made, and if you wanted to be lazy and not go for it, I was. Besides." He scowled at me and Alek. "I was sick and tired of trying to bring their fucking Bratva down."

"You idiot!" Dom thrust his gun out again, reclaiming Murphy's attention.

I looked at Becca again, wishing she could see the desperate hope in my eyes. That she could understand that we just had to see how this would play out. If Alek or I reached for our guns, they'd shoot us first.

Patience, sweetheart. Please. Trust me and be patient.

"My mistress died from that shit," Dom shouted. "My favorite mistress, a lover like no other. That crap *killed* her!"

"Not my problem." Murphy shook his head. "I just want my half of the drugs and we'll call it even."

"No!" Dom stepped forward, closer to Becca, but stared at Murphy. "I want to wash my hands of it all. I want that shit secured—on my property and under my control. I need to concentrate on building up my family and focusing on the Rossini name and power before going after any rivals." He spared us a disdainful glance.

"You're not getting anything from me," Murphy yelled as he lifted his gun higher.

A well-honed instinct was all the premonition I needed.

I lunged, diving for Becca just as they fired at each other. I crashed to the cement floor, rolling to take the brunt of the impact and move her to safety, out of the range of gunfire.

She gripped me, holding me close as we slammed to a stop against the wall. I braced my hand on the back of her head, cushioning the blow, and once we hit the surface, I breathed through the hard hit.

She lay in my arms, patting at me frantically. "Were you—Are you —Were you hit?"

I shook my head, looking her over and also checking for any blood or wounds.

"He was," Alek answered from the middle of the room. He kicked Dom's shoe, proving that the Mafia Don was indeed dead. A bullet clean through the head would do that, a clean shot right between his eyes.

Becca gagged, scrambling to stand and get away from her rapist, now a body to be disposed of. I held her hands, helping her up and keeping myself between her and Murphy.

Alek had his gun trained on him as he walked closer, and as I shielded Becca, I raised my gun as well.

"You stupid bitch!" he roared. Struggling to sit up, he showed us his blood-stained shirt, soaking from Dom's shot.

As soon as Murphy pointed his gun at his daughter, at the woman I loved, I lifted my firearm and shot once.

Becca gasped, clutching me and burying her face against my chest.

Murphy slumped back to the ground, lifeless and finally dead.

No longer a problem.

I'd done what I originally promised my brothers that I would do.

Take out this asshole.

Murphy was dead. So was Dom. My hit list was getting damned short, but as I hugged Becca and rubbed her back, I caught Alek smiling at us together.

If there were ever a time to scratch off the names of my enemies and lessen my workload in terms of keeping the Bratva safe, it was now.

Because I intended to give this woman and our future my all.

"Is it over?" Becca asked, timid and nervous as she fisted the front of my shirt and hid from looking at the dead men.

I nodded, turning her and tipping her chin up. "They're done." I lowered my lips to hers, demanding and gruff in needing her sweet taste. She hesitated at first, perhaps so stunned by what just happened. Within a moment, though, she replied in kind, pushing up to me and kissing me back hungrily.

Her heart raced with mine.

Her soft curves molded and fit against me.

And I opened my mouth wider, insisting on a deeper kiss to match the intensity of relief that I could feel now.

But you and I are just starting.

32

BECCA

As I walked through the vacation villa the day after Dom and Murphy tried to end each other over the long-term plan I'd overheard them dissolving so long ago, I realized how much of that night ended up being a blur.

I supposed it was my mind's way of protecting me, shading all the details into a hazy recollection so I wouldn't dwell in the trauma of all that passed.

I wasn't in denial. Dom was dead. So was Murphy. And I didn't mourn either of them. Not one bit.

Everything in the present seemed so surreal, though, and I wondered when I would feel confident in what to do next.

Ivan had told me that he wanted me in his life, but now that it seemed like the rest of my life was actually going to start, he was making himself scarce again. I got it. I knew he was busy with his brothers, tending to the aftermath of all that violence. Mafia men, as I'd come to learn, were busy individuals.

Yet, I felt lost.

I was no longer here as a hostage. Steven was dead and would never need to be baited or lured to come out of hiding again.

I was free of his influence.

I was no longer a guest here, either. Since Ivan and I admitted the depth of our feelings for each other, after he asked me to move into his room with him, I felt like a girlfriend. A mistress? Something with intimacy but not so casual that we were roommates.

It would be far easier to understand what I was supposed to do now if he were around to speak with me, so it was with a mixture of giddiness and anxiety when I heard him come in through the front door.

"Hello?"

The guards were no longer as present. Margie, too, had left to help Mila and Amy at the mansion in the city.

Yet, here I was. Unlabeled, lost, and a lot in love.

I'd faced so many changes of late, but the one that I had yet to come to terms with was the evidence of my pregnancy. I found a test in one of the guest wings, and sure enough, it lit up positive right away.

Telling Ivan was critical. I had to. But I didn't know how or when.

He'd told me that I'd changed his views on having a kid or starting a family, but he didn't strike me as a family man through and through. Perhaps he'd said that in the heat of the moment.

What if he thinks I'm trying to trap him with a baby?

Too many unknowns resided in my head, and as I headed to the front door to greet him, I tried my hardest to stick with the things I did know.

In Ivan, I'd finally found that man who would care for me as I was, a good, hardworking, and honest hero who didn't want to use me for his own gains.

"Becca?" he called out as he strode down the hallway.

My feet were slow. I was sluggish to approach him with my news.

"Hi," I replied, trying to smile as he came into view.

"I was—"

Emily cried out, and I sighed, wishing I could've had an uninter-rupted chance to speak with him now that he was here and we were alone.

He chuckled, walking with me to her door. Still lagging with the indecision of how to break the news to Ivan, I lingered near the window, looking out as he beat me to her.

"Hey, quiet." He still used those direct requests, but he was gentle and soft with her.

She looked perfect in his arms, calming against his chest and glancing at me.

"No need to fuss. We're right here."

I swallowed hard, overwhelmed with the picture-perfect moment of him holding her so carefully and with ease.

"Well, she'll need to get used to the concept of competing for attention soon. She'll have to let her sibling fuss too."

Oh, shit. Of the stupidest, lamest ways to break the news...

I couldn't believe I'd just blurted it out like that. My cheeks heated and I bit my lip, worrying. Doubts abounded.

Ivan paused in rocking Emily, gazing at me with an intense blend of shock and awe.

"Becca?"

I sighed. "I'm pregnant."

He raised his brows. "Wow."

"And that's not all."

He widened his eyes, already stunned but bracing for more.

"I've fallen for you, Ivan. And I love you. I loved you before you saved me yesterday, and I'll love you for the rest of our days, too. I miss you every minute that you're gone or busy, and I constantly wonder if you think about me too. Those are the truest things that I *know* right now when I have zero direction of where to go and what to do."

He let me catch my breath, rocking Emily.

My home was gone. All my things were sold or taken to the trash when I never came back. My artwork was all ruined, save for the one notebook I'd sketched in here at the vacation house. And even my little studio was trashed. My grandmother's space was destroyed, and I bet it was Steven, seeking my artwork for those drugs.

All along, I was literally the bait. Both Steven and Dom had wanted me to smuggle their drugs in my artwork, and because of both of them, I was rootless.

"After all that's gone down, all I have to guide me is the reassurance that I still have Emily in my life. And this baby inside me." I pressed my hand to my flat stomach. "And my love for you."

His gaze softened, darkening with adoration as he stepped up close to me. Emily slept once more, lax in his arms, and he got in my face.

"That's not all you have, sweetheart." He leaned down to kiss my lips, hard and incessant with that taste of need I was addicted to.

"I'm sorry things have been busy, but I wanted to make it a smooth transition when you and Emily move into my home in the city."

My heart soared. I smiled, hoping he was serious.

"You'll always have my love."

I reached up and pulled him down for a deeper kiss.

"And it will never, ever be conditional." He narrowed his eyes playfully. "Do you understand?"

"From the bottom of my heart," I replied, sealing it with another kiss.

33

IVAN

*ne month later...*

I adjusted Emily in my arms as I checked my phone.

Alek had texted me again, and I sighed. With Murphy dead and the Rossinis minding their own business, we didn't have anything crazy happening. *For now.* I wasn't so deluded as to think peace would last for good. The peace Becca and I were finding together wouldn't last long, either. It seemed that having "two under two" would be a challenging trial, but at least we would have staggered ages between our kids. Nik and Amy would have two babies at the same time any day now.

Alek: *I think Maxim feels left out.*

I rolled my eyes, following Becca through the studio space.

"What?" she insisted playfully, looking back at me. "Why'd you roll your eyes like that? Don't you think those windows look lopsided?"

I smiled at her. "I was checking in with Alek." Then I furrowed my brow. "And no, they're not lopsided." I bumped her hip, making her step off the thick rug. "You were lopsided."

She made a silly face at me, walking around and checking out the studio property I wanted to buy for her. If it suited her needs. And if it checked her preferences.

"Da, Da, Da, Da." Emily babbled away in my arms, filling me with so much joy that she was already identifying me as her daddy.

Just yesterday, I got the papers of official adoption, and I would never forget the soulful euphoria of knowing I really had a daughter.

Alek: *He's mentioned it three times now.*

Alek: *That he thinks he doesn't do enough for the family.*

I shook my head. He always did. Our youngest brother was more of a behind-the-scenes man, but he was important. He'd moved from doing bookkeeping under our uncle to all kinds of administrative tasks for Alek. He knew how to fight like the rest of us. He stepped up to be backup as needed. I'd forever be grateful for his help tracking Becca when Dom took her from that sex club.

Alek: *I think he's hoping for something more dangerous.*

I let Emily down to toddle after Becca in this wide-open space.

Ivan: *Or maybe he wants to be trusted with a job or mission on his own.*

Ivan: *Assign him to something so he can get a taste of what it's like out there.*

Alek: *I think I know exactly what to assign him to.*

I huffed a laugh, pocketing my phone. *Then why ask me?*

"Something wrong?" Becca asked, holding Emily's hand as she approached me.

"No. Just brother stuff."

She grinned. "Ah."

I draped my arm around her shoulders and kissed her temple. "So, a no on this place?"

She nodded. "It just doesn't feel right. And kind of far from home."

Home, as in the brand-new apartment we'd chosen together. It seemed smarter to start over in a new place, not the penthouse where I'd first taken her. Where we lived hardly mattered to me, just as long as it was with her and Emily, with room to grow.

"Ready for the appointment?" I asked, grinning.

She nodded. "Are you sure you want to find out the gender?" she teased.

"Oh, yeah."

We headed straight there to the private office of the doctor handling Mila's and Amy's pregnancies. Dr. Francis was a busy lady with all of us, and I looked forward to seeing all our kids running around together, raised in a full family setting.

After we checked in with the receptionist, I set Emily on my knees and bounced her to entertain her.

"You're going to be the best dad in the world," Becca said as she rested her head on my shoulder. Her red hair tumbled down, and Emily giggled, reaching out to grab it.

"I already am," I corrected her.

She leaned up to kiss me. "That's right. I still can't believe the adoption papers came so quickly."

That's how things work in the family. The documents were legitimate, but we had our ways of bribing for speedier outcomes. That didn't hold true here, though, as we waited for the ultrasound appointment well past its scheduled spot.

"Sorry!" Dr. Francis said twenty more minutes later. "Babies. They never go according to *my* schedule." She winked at Becca as she moved the wand over her belly. As she asked her a few questions about her pregnancy with Emily, I focused on distracting Emily from wanting to wander and climb in here.

"You're sure you want to know?" the doctor asked after she confirmed the baby was growing appropriately. I had to give her credit. Not once did she slip with a pronoun when she pointed out all the measurements and whatnot.

I nodded. "I am."

Becca took my hand. "Me too."

"You see this here?" Dr. Francis pointed to a shape on the screen. I didn't want to admit it, but I still had no clue what I was looking at on that contrasted image.

"Is that a penis?" Becca exclaimed.

"Penis!" Emily parroted.

I shook my head, laughing as I hugged her close.

Becca laughed. "Emily!"

"It's a boy?" I checked, already getting ahead of myself, thinking of names, wondering what sports we'd play first, if he'd have Becca's red hair...

A son!

She nodded. "Yep. You've got a healthy baby boy. Congratulations."

I stared at the image while Dr. Francis cleaned up the gel on Becca's stomach. After the doctor left, seeking her assistant to arrange Becca's next appointment dates, I gazed at my woman and smiled.

I saw the rest of my life in her warm stare of love.

"I'm the luckiest fucking man alive," I said.

She widened her eyes, sitting up and covering Emily's ears.

I smirked. Like she wouldn't hear profanity sooner or later.

"A daughter." I kissed Emily's curls. "A son." I leaned down and kissed Becca's stomach. "How about you be my wife and we'll be a complete family?"

Her jaw dropped. "Was that...? Are you proposing?"

I nodded and pulled the ring from my pocket. Emily reached for it, but I was quicker, slipping in on Becca's finger and feeling smug that it was a perfect fit.

Just like she was in my life.

Grinning, she leaned up and kissed me. "Okay," she said against my lips.

"I swear I'll love you forever, Becca Valkov."

It had a much nicer ring to it than Murphy.

"No matter what," she promised right back, "I'll love you, too."